Who Killed
the Robins Family?

19/50 .

CONTEST

How to enter the WHO KILLED THE ROBINS FAMILY? competition:

You have to answer FIVE questions about each of the EIGHT members of the Robins family – Tyler Robins, Evelyn Robins, Marshall Robins, Libby (Robins) Pittman, Lewis Robins, James Robins, Cynthia Robins and Candace Robins.

At the head of each set of five answers, put the name of the victim: for example, TYLER. Then answer the first 4 questions precisely and the 5th question as concisely as possible, but in not more than 100 words. You may use a separate piece of paper for each 'victim' if you wish.

The questions in each case are:
1. Who was the killer?
2. Where did the murder take place?
3. When did the murder happen?
4. How was the victim killed?
5. Why was the victim killed?

Answer all 5 questions in the order given (remember to identify each victim clearly) for each family member. Print or type your answers, making sure that your name and address is clearly printed at the top of each page.

Enter the competition as many times as you like but each entry must be posted in a separate envelope and ACCOMPANIED BY AN ENTRY FORM. Each book contains an entry form and entry forms can also be found in the *Daily Express*. Answers submitted without an entry form are automatically disqualified.

The correct answers, as determined by the authors, are based on clues found in the book. These answers are being held in a sealed vault pending the closing date of

RULES

the competition. In the case of more than one (or no) completely correct solution, the winning entry will be determined by the best set of answers to the question 'Why was the victim killed?'.

Best answers to this question (in each case) will be determined first by correctness. The answers (in not more than 100 words) will then be evaluated on the basis of logic, clarity of expression, creativity and neatness.

A panel of expert celebrities will judge the contest and every entry will be examined. The judges will award the £10,000 prize to the sender of what they consider to be the best entry. The decision of this panel will be final, and no correspondence can be entered into.

The competition is open to anyone aged 18 and over, except for employees of Michael Joseph Ltd, and Express Newspapers PLC and their families.

Proof of posting cannot be accepted as proof of delivery, and no responsibility can be accepted for entries lost, delayed or damaged, before or after delivery. Entries are the property of Michael Joseph Ltd.

Send your entry to: Daily Express
WHO KILLED THE ROBINS
FAMILY? competition
4 Racquet Court
London EC88 1BB
to arrive not later than APRIL 15, 1984.

Only entries with complete answers to all five questions for each victim are eligible for the £10,000 prize.

The winner will be notified by post on or before May 2, 1984. The winner and winning solution will be announced on May 28, 1984.

ENTRY FORM

I enclose my solution to the WHO KILLED THE ROBINS
FAMILY? competition

NAME ....

ADDRESS ....

....

Post to: The Daily Express
WHO KILLED THE ROBINS FAMILY?
competition
4 Racquet Court
London EC88 1BB

Who Killed
the Robins Family?

Created by Bill Adler
Written by Thomas Chastain

Michael Joseph
LONDON

First published in Great Britain by
Michael Joseph Limited
44 Bedford Square
London W.C.1
1983

ISBN 0 7181 2373 5

Filmset by
Cambrian Typesetters, Aldershot, Hants.
Printed in Great Britain by
Richard Clay (The Chaucer Press) Ltd,
Bungay, Suffolk

For
Leonard Franklin –
WHO BROUGHT US TOGETHER

AUTHORS' NOTE

The enigma of who killed the Robins family — and where and when and why and how they died — is, as are all murder mysteries, essentially a puzzle. There are, of course, more pieces to the puzzle than fit. But the pieces that *do* fit are all included in this account of the circumstances of their deaths.

Part of the challenge of constructing, and of solving, puzzles is that they not be too easy. This is especially true of fictional murder mysteries where words, which lead us, or mislead us, through the maze of the plot become the pieces of the puzzle. It becomes a matter of separating out all those facts that, when put together with other facts, do not add up to a logical solution of the mysteries contained in the account *and* of putting together all those facts that do.

As any experienced reader of fictional murder mysteries knows, all such works are basically variations on a form that has been set long since — from the murder inside the locked room to the trail of the 'red herrings'. A reader who keeps this in mind and catches the echoes of, and references to, some past fictional murder mysteries will have an advantage.

Finally, *not every single piece of information*

needed to solve who killed the eight members of the Robins family — and where and when and why and how they died — is contained in these pages. But the clues that will lead the reader to such information are all here.

So, reader, you cannot say, as has many a character in many a Gothic novel, 'If only I had known . . .'

BILL ADLER
THOMAS CHASTAIN
New York City

CAST OF CHARACTERS
(IN ORDER OF APPEARANCE)

TYLER ROBINS — Patriarch of the family; president and chairman of the board of the multimillion-dollar family-owned Robins Cosmetics.

EVELYN ROBINS — Wife of Tyler for forty years; overseer of their various properties — including the Maryland estate, Greenlawn — and their six children.

MARSHALL ROBINS — Eldest of the children; separated from his wife, Pamela, after the birth of one daughter; has proved to be a disappointment to his father.

LIBBY (ROBINS) PITTMAN — First-born of the daughters; works in the Robins Cosmetics laboratories in New Jersey; married to George Pittman.

LEWIS ROBINS — A bachelor; commutes between Robins Cosmetics jobs in Toronto and the New York City headquarters of the company.

JAMES ROBINS — Aged twenty-six, youngest of the sons; works in the Paris office of Robins

Cosmetics; is married to a French beauty, Geneviève.

THE TWINS:

CYNTHIA ROBINS — Lives with her twin sister in London where both work for Robins Cosmetics; unmarried; the twins, twenty-three years old, are the youngest of the children.

CANDACE ROBINS — Inseparable from her twin all their lives; a mirror image of her beautiful sister except for a tiny dark mole on Candace's left cheek.

ALFRED WALES — The Robins family butler.

DORINA WALES — The Robins family cook-housekeeper, wife of Alfred.

PAMELA ROBINS — Wife of Marshall, mother of his daughter.

PHILLIP WINGATE — Lives in London; has captivated Cynthia.

JANICE ELGAR — A guest on the ill-fated cruise taken by certain members of the Robins family.

PAUL BRYCE — A guest on the same cruise; a business competitor of Tyler Robins.

DR JOHN FORBES — A former beau of Evelyn's; present Robins family physician.

IAN SHEFFIELD — Captain aboard the Robins family yacht, *Falconer*.

PERCIVAL – Steward aboard the *Falconer*.

ARTURO – Cook aboard the *Falconer*.

JULIAN SHIELDS – Close friend and Robins family lawyer.

B. J. GRIEG – A private detective in Manhattan.

GEORGE PITTMAN – Husband of Libby; package designer for Robins Cosmetics.

GENEVIEVE ROBINS – Wife of James; will give birth to their first child.

AVA WINGATE – Lives in London; sister [*sic*] of Phillip.

SERGEANT HORGAN – Homicide sergeant with the Maryland State Police.

STEVEN BOLAND – Englishman who has become obsessed with Candace.

JOACHIM – Magician of extraordinary ability who was born deaf.

GENET – Young Eurasian girl; assistant to Joachim in his magic acts.

LENA BRAM – Spiritualist; conducts séance in London.

HENRY FOWLES – A private investigator in London.

ROBERT COVINGTON — Inspector, New Scotland Yard, London.

MARGARET CARMODY — Maid in the New Jersey home of the George Pittmans.

WILLIAM RAYLOR — Homicide detective with the New Jersey police.

ERNEST TRUAX — Works in new products development for Robins Cosmetics.

AGNES ELLSWORTH — Spinster neighbour of the Pittmans in New Jersey.

TONY SPADUA — Burglar; arrested by police in New Jersey.

CAPTAIN WALTHAM — Captain in the homicide division of the Maryland State Police.

PROLOGUE

For those seeking a single thread which would connect the bizarre series of murders of the eight members of the Robins family, there is none. That they were a family of great wealth was only a casual factor in the chain of events.

The last time they would all be together alive was on a day in early summer when they gathered for a reunion at Greenlawn, the sprawling family estate in the Green Spring Valley of Maryland.

From early morning on that day, the six Robins offspring — three men and three women — had begun arriving from around the country and around the world. The occasion they were there to celebrate was the fortieth wedding anniversary of their parents, Tyler and Evelyn Robins. Some of the Robins children were married and one, Marshall, had a child of his own, but it was family tradition that certain special reunions, such as this one, be limited to the eight of them.

Tyler Robins, sixty-one years old at the time, was a large, robust man with a direct, forceful manner who looked six to eight years younger than his true age. He was president and chairman of the board of the family-owned Robins Cosmetics, a multimillion-dollar business ranking among the first twenty of *Fortune* 500 companies, with offices around the world. The company's headquarters was in New York City, and Tyler and Evelyn also had a town house on East Fiftieth Street in Manhattan.

Evelyn Robins was two years younger than her husband, a graceful, slender woman who was still noticed by most men wherever she went. Before she met and married Tyler Robins, Evelyn had had the romantic notion that perhaps one day she would write poetry or novels. She had long since given up any thought of such endeavours but she did keep a daily diary. One of her entries for that day of the reunion read:

> The children are all here now. As always when I observe them carefully for the first time after we've been apart for a while, I am struck by the same curious fact. Yes, that there is much likeness of me and of Tyler in them — and yet, how much too, they appear as strangers to me. As if the children I raised who were so familiar to me as gentle Marshall, busy James, solemn Lewis, so-serious Libby and oh, those adorable peas-in-a-pod twins, Cynthia and Candace, had vanished somewhere back in time. And, fanciful as it sounds, that their names had been taken by these adult impersonators I see today. I wonder if other parents ever have this feeling about their grown children? I wonder if Tyler does? I would like to ask him. But, of course, he would just dismiss it as silly nonsense on my part. . . .

'Wealth,' Tyler had frequently admonished his

children, 'does not make you better than those who do not have it — unless you prove yourself so. That, I expect you always to try to do.'

To this end, Tyler had seen to it that all six of them had the most expensive, if not always the best, education money could buy. After their schooling was finished, he brought each of them into Robins Cosmetics, sometimes deliberately pitting them one against another to see which one would be likely to succeed him when he retired from the company.

Marshall, at thirty-four the eldest of the children, had proved the biggest disappointment to his father. Although, ironically enough, Marshall of all the children most resembled his father in looks, he lacked Tyler's drive, ambition, and shrewdness. Marshall had not married until four years earlier. Tyler had approved of the girl, Pamela; indeed, he had introduced them. But two years after the marriage, and after the birth of a daughter, Marshall and Pamela had separated. Marshall, who had been working in the company's New York headquarters, had asked for a transfer elsewhere until he and Pamela decided whether or not they would divorce. Tyler had sent him to manage Robins Cosmetics' Los Angeles office.

Libby, the first-born of the Robins daughters, two years younger than Marshall, worked in the Robins Cosmetics laboratories in Mercer County, New Jersey. Her job was in new products development. Libby had much of her mother's graceful attractiveness. She had married a package designer who also worked at the Robins laboratories and the marriage was a good one. Libby and her husband, George Pittman — there were no children as yet — lived in a large white Colonial-style house in Princeton, New Jersey.

Tyler and Evelyn's second son, Lewis, was thirty-one years old. Still a bachelor, he had degrees in science and chemistry, and worked in the Toronto office of Robins Cosmetics three days a week and in the New York headquarters the other two days, commuting back and forth between the two cities. A quiet, hard-working man who had the slender build of his mother, Lewis led a more solitary life than the other members of the busy family. So far, he had resisted all match-making plans attempted by his father and mother and well-meaning friends.

The remaining son, James, twenty-six at the time of the reunion in Maryland, had more of his father's aggressive personality and forcefulness than did the other children. He also tended to be impatient and impulsive, traits that Tyler hoped would be tempered with time. Still, Tyler had not tried to discourage him when James requested transfers from one Robins Cosmetics office to another, working in six different offices within a year. The reason for his restlessness around that time was his involvement in an affair that would have led to his disinheritance had Tyler Robins known about it. The affair was with the daughter of Alfred and Dorina Wales, a couple who had worked as butler and housekeeper for the family ever since Tyler and Evelyn had first married. Their daughter, Carrie, and James had grown up together, had had an affair, and she had had his child, leaving Greenlawn before the birth of the baby. Only Alfred, Dorina, and Evelyn — who had made all the financial arrangements for the girl's welfare — had been told of the circumstances. Both the butler and the housekeeper kept quiet, knowing that they had no other choice. Still, it is possible that they hoped the two would be able to marry someday.

For the past two years James had worked in the Paris office of Robins Cosmetics. James, a dark, intense man, was now married to a French beauty, Geneviève. She, only a year out of her teens when she and James married, would have their first child before the year was ended.

The youngest of the Robins children were the twins, Cynthia and Candace, who were twenty-three years old and beauties themselves. Mirror images of one another, the twins had been inseparable all their lives and remained almost impossible to tell apart except that Candace had a tiny dark mole on her left cheek. The two lived together in a flat in London where they worked in the British offices of Robins Cosmetics, Cynthia in advertising, Candace in public relations.

Tyler Robins enjoyed playing the role of squire when he was at Greenlawn. That summer day he was up early and, dressed in boots and jodhpurs, out inspecting the grounds, the stables, the tennis courts, and the swimming pool.

Once the eight of them were together they spent the day riding on horseback through the rolling hills of the estate, playing tennis, and splashing in the pool.

That evening they gathered around the dining-room table and there were champagne toasts by the children to Tyler and Evelyn, followed by polite applause from the butler, Alfred, the two serving maids in attendance, and Alfred's wife, the housekeeper, Dorina, who came in from the kitchen. During dinner the pleasant discussion centered on the extended cruise Tyler and Evelyn would be taking next week on the family yacht. Marshall and the twins would be going with them, along with other, non-family guests.

The first of the eight murders of the Robins family would occur on this cruise.

CHAPTER ONE

I

Not many days after the family reunion in Maryland, the Robins' yacht, *Falconer*, embarked from Honolulu on a course southwestward through the Pacific Ocean.

The yacht carried a crew of nine — including the cook and one steward — in addition to the captain, Ian Sheffield. There were ten passenger cabins aboard. On deck there was a shuffleboard court and, in the stern, gear for deep-sea fishing. The captain and crew had their quarters on the second level below deck.

Normally the diesel-powered *Falconer* was berthed in Wilmington, Delaware. For this particular cruise, Tyler had instructed the captain and crew to have the yacht waiting in Honolulu for boarding. It was there when Tyler, Evelyn, Marshall, the twins, and the guests Tyler had invited jetted into Hawaii. Tyler's quixotic idea had been to make a Pacific cruise from Honolulu to Wake Island, where he had served in World War II and which he had never visited since.

Tyler had assembled a curious mixture of guests — five of them — for the cruise.

1

The biggest surprise to Marshall Robins was the appearance of his estranged wife, Pamela. She was a young woman who would have been plain-looking except that she had managed to create for herself a certain air of chic stylishness through her selection of fashionable dress and application of cosmetics.

Tyler took Marshall aside that day and, speaking firmly, said, 'I want you to give your marriage another chance, young man. This cruise will provide the opportunity. I expect you to make an effort to see if you and Pamela can make a go of things again. Do you understand?'

Marshall was furious with his father's meddling but, knowing they were going to be confined to close quarters for the next several weeks, nodded his head and said nothing.

Cynthia Robins had been equally surprised when Phillip Wingate had appeared at the yacht on the day of departure.

For the past several months she had been dating Wingate in London and had become deeply enamoured of him. She hadn't realised that any of her family — except her twin — even knew of the existence of Wingate. And now here he was, a guest invited by her father.

Phillip Wingate, who was English, was a good ten years older than Cynthia, a solidly built man, blond with a blond moustache, and handsome enough if one didn't look too closely and note the faint lines of dissolution beginning to show beneath the surface of his face.

Wingate was distressed when he discovered that Cynthia had not expected him to be on the cruise. He had assumed when he received the

2

invitation from Tyler that it had been Cynthia's idea because she felt the time had come for him to meet her family. Nevertheless, he attempted to carry the incident off with aplomb, saying it was extraordinarily thoughtful of Tyler Robins to invite him.

Cynthia could only nod her head.

The other female guest Tyler had invited was a stranger to the members of the Robins family aboard the yacht. Tyler had introduced her as Janice Elgar, the widow of a friend of his in London, Frederick Elgar. She was a tall, slim woman with raven hair who appeared to be not much older than the Robins twins.

The remaining two guests were known to the Robins family.

Paul Bryce was a longtime friendly competitor of Tyler's in the cosmetics field. Bryce, a jovial, big-boned man, was around the same age as Tyler, and was chairman of the board of Tiempo Cosmetics. He had been eager to go on the cruise because of the opportunity he would have to do some deep-sea fishing, a favourite sport of his.

The fifth guest was John Forbes, Dr John Forbes, who had been the family physician as well as friend for years. In fact, Forbes had been Evelyn Robins's beau at the time Tyler had first met Evelyn and swept her off her feet and into marriage. It was typical of the way Tyler operated in life that as soon as he and Evelyn were married, he would choose John Forbes to be their family doctor. Forbes had remained a bachelor and, although he tried to keep his feelings hidden, was clearly still in love with Evelyn. Ageing — he was now sixty years old — had given him a look of

3

distinction, his hair more silver than brown, his face unlined except for the crinkles around his eyes.

During the first week after the *Falconer* left Honolulu, life on board took on a routine that was seldom to vary for the rest of the voyage.

In the mornings members of the party would eat breakfast at different times, each of them free to rise as early or as late as they liked. Then the men would usually take turns at trying their luck at deep-sea fishing, and sometimes the women would join in. Tyler caught a four-foot marlin, Evelyn caught a shark, and Marshall brought up a three-foot sailfish. There were also games of shuffleboard in the mornings, and sun-bathing.

The midday meals were served on deck, smörgåsbord-style.

In the afternoons the sun was so hot that almost everyone stayed indoors or in the shade on deck.

The women sometimes took siestas or played gin rummy in one or another of the cabins. And every afternoon the men played poker in the main saloon where Alfred, the Robins butler, served them drinks. Even though the yacht carried a steward, Tyler had brought Alfred along for the cruise.

In the evenings, all the members of the family and the guests were expected to be present at dinner in the main saloon. After dinner they would play word games, or Alfred would show a movie on the yacht's projector.

The weather stayed fair day after day, and on an afternoon in the second week of the cruise, Candace came up from her cabin to find her mother alone on deck.

Candace flopped into a deck chair next to her mother's and asked with an exasperated sigh, 'Mother, why does he do things like this?'

Evelyn put down the Agatha Christie mystery novel she was reading, pushed her sunglasses up so they rested on top of her head, and looked at her daughter.

'Why does who do things like what?' she asked gently.

Candace made an impatient gesture with her hand. 'You know perfectly well who and what I mean. *Father*, and the way he invited poor Pamela and Phillip Wingate and not a word beforehand to Marshall or Cynthia, or any of us. I think the last person on earth Marshall wanted to see was Pamela, much less spend several weeks with her. And Cynthia's absolutely mortified that Phillip Wingate's been put into such an awkward situation.'

Evelyn patted her daughter's arm. 'I expect you know exactly why your father invited both of them. He wants to keep Pamela in the family and' — she paused and then went on — 'and to learn more about Mr Wingate.'

'But how did he know about Phillip Wingate?' Candace asked. 'I was the only one in the family who knew Cynthia was seeing him and I certainly didn't tell Father.'

Evelyn shook her head. 'When will you children ever learn that you can't keep secrets from your father, not with all the resources he has at his command?'

'And what about the others he invited? Who is that woman, Janice Elgar? And why did he invite that man, Bryce?'

5

'You left out John Forbes,' Evelyn said, smiling. 'The answer to your question, I daresay, is that your father had a reason for inviting every one of them. And, unless I am wrong, he'll make his reasons known to them before this cruise is over.'

Tyler Robins was to prove the truth of his wife's words over the following weeks.

In fact — after the murder — a variety of sources would provide a record of much of what transpired aboard the *Falconer* during those weeks at sea.

There would be Marshall Robins's testimony at the U.S. Coast Guard inquiry, sometime later, when he would say: 'Yes, it's true that during the whole voyage Father kept at me and kept at me to resume my marriage with Pamela. As for the night in question, when others heard our raised voices in my cabin, yes, we did have a heated argument. I tried to explain to him that, no matter what Pamela told him, she didn't *love* me. But he wouldn't listen. He got very angry, and that's when he told me that if I didn't patch up my marriage with Pamela, he was going to cut me out of his will. And he was going to leave my share of the estate to my daughter, his granddaughter. . . . No, I did not kill my father. . . . No, I do not know who killed him. . . .'

The existence of a tape recording, secretly made by Tyler, of a conversation between Tyler and Paul Bryce would be discovered:

TYLER: Paul, I have a — ah — rather delicate matter I want to discuss with you.
BRYCE: Go ahead, let's hear it.

6

TYLER: It concerns dealings you have had with Ernest Truax.

BRYCE: Who? I don't know what —

TYLER: Ernest Truax, my employee. Come on, Paul, let's not play games. I have documents, photographs, proving you made pay-offs to Truax to buy information on new products Robins Cosmetics has developed. I hired an investigator. I have the proof of what you've been doing.

BRYCE: I don't want to discuss this —

TYLER: There's nothing to discuss. If I took you to court, it would all come out; you'd be ruined. I have another solution.

BRYCE: Look, Tyler, I am not going to discuss this —

TYLER: The solution is that you will pay me five million dollars, off the books, and that'll be the end of the matter. You have a choice, one or the other. And you have until the end of the cruise to decide which it'll be. Now, let's have another drink. Pass me your glass . . .

Evelyn Robins would, one night during these weeks, write in her diary:

John Forbes just visited with me a few minutes ago and told me of a most odd and disturbing conversation he says Tyler had with him. John says Tyler told him that he, Tyler, had reason to believe I was having an affair with someone! Poor John says he was absolutely flabbergasted

7

— and particularly when, he says, Tyler slyly intimated that he thought John was the one I was having the affair with! This is certainly turning into a strange cruise. What next?

Tyler Robins would leave behind a letter he was composing to his daughter Cynthia, which he never finished and never gave to her:

My dear Daughter:
This is a most difficult letter for me to write and I do it only because of my great concern for you and your future happiness. As you can guess from those foregoing words, it concerns your friend Phillip Wingate. When I first learned of your interest in him (and you need not concern yourself with how I learned this), I had a discreet investigation conducted into his background and affairs. And while this investigation is still incomplete, several disquieting facts about him have turned up. As you know — he has made no secret of it — he is a widower, and the antique business he now runs in London and the small estate where he lives in Meadlands with his sister were inherited from his dead wife. What you don't know, nor do many others, is that his wife died under rather mysterious circumstances. An unexplained fall. The case is still open in the files of Scotland Yard. As you have perhaps noted in past days, Wingate becomes quite edgy and ill at ease when in my company. That is because I have dropped vague hints to him intimating that I may know more about him than he thinks. Then, there is another reason for his uneasiness on this cruise. The woman, Janice Elgar, who is on board. The investigator I hired to look into

8

Wingate's past discovered her. Wingate's dead wife was her aunt. She is suspicious of the role Wingate might have played in her aunt's death. Since Janice was still a youngster at the time Wingate last saw her, he has so far failed to recognize her. Yet, as you may have observed, something about Janice puzzles him. Yes, I am playing a game of cat and mouse with him — and he knows it. If he is innocent of any wrongdoing, well, no harm done. But if I find out otherwise, all I can say is, God help him!!! I expect to receive more news about him by ship's radio from London in a few days. When I do I shall complete this letter and give it to you. . . .

There would also be the testimony of Alfred, the Robins butler, at the U.S. Coast Guard inquiry sometime later, when he would say: 'Yes, it's true that Mr Tyler Robins had a run-in with Captain Sheffield and the cook and steward of the *Falconer*. It had to do with the matter of the disappearance of a case of scotch whisky from the ship's storeroom. I was the one who discovered that the case of liquor was missing and I promptly reported the fact to Mr Robins. He then called in the other three — they were the only other persons beside myself who had keys to the storeroom — and questioned them. All three denied any knowledge of the missing liquor. It's true there was a heated exchange among the four of them. Mr Robins then informed them that unless he uncovered exactly who had taken the case of liquor, he would fire all three of them at the end of the cruise. . . . Yes, I would have to say that there were bitter feelings among the four of them — that is, Captain

9

Sheffield; the cook, Arturo; the steward, Percival; and Mr Robins, from then on. . . .'

All of these incidents, about which the above records remained, occurred before the fateful day aboard the *Falconer*.

This day, unlike those that had preceded it on the voyage, dawned dark and stormy, with a heavy rain falling and the seas running high and rough, as if the elements themselves were setting the stage for the deadly drama to come.

Most of the passengers stayed later than usual in their cabins before going to breakfast in the main saloon. Afterward, most of them remained in the saloon, exchanging remarks and reassurances about the weather.

Tyler Robins was the exception. He was up at dawn, had a light breakfast, and then went to the bridge where he conferred with the captain about the storm.

'No trouble now,' Captain Sheffield informed him. 'But from the weather reports we've been getting, the storm may worsen before we pass through it.'

Tyler took this news to those in the saloon, trying to cheer them up by saying, 'The *Falconer*'s a seaworthy craft. There's no need for any of you to worry.'

At Tyler's suggestion, Alfred put a movie on the projector and the other passengers settled down to watch.

Throughout the morning, Tyler divided his time between the bridge, the main saloon, and his cabin.

He was keeping a log of the trip and at one point before noon, he wrote:

10

Thursday — a bad storm. Captain says we'll be all right but there's rough weather ahead. Everyone bearing up okay so far . . .

At noon, a light lunch was served in the main saloon, with all of the passengers present. When lunch was finished, Tyler suggested that the men play their usual game of poker. The women retired to their cabins to read or play gin rummy.

In mid-afternoon Alfred brought a tray of drinks and a box of cigars to the saloon, and passed the drinks around the table. Later, it would be remembered that Tyler and Paul Bryce had orange juice and champagne, Marshall had a bullshot, Dr John Forbes had a Bloody Mary, and Phillip Wingate had a vodka and tonic.

Less than an hour after the drinks were served, Tyler complained of not feeling well. He continued to play for a while longer, however, until he broke out in a cold sweat and had to leave the table, unsteady on his feet.

Dr Forbes, concerned about him, accompanied him to his cabin and made him stretch out on the bunk. Tyler complained that he had severe stomach pains and felt feverish. Dr Forbes took Tyler's temperature and checked his pulse. Both were slightly elevated. Dr Forbes suggested that he rest quietly for a while, said he would be back shortly, and hurried away to inform Evelyn that Tyler was feeling ill.

Evelyn then went to her husband's cabin and sat with him for a time.

A short while later Paul Bryce, too, complained of feeling ill. Dr Forbes found that Bryce's temperature and pulse were slightly elevated. He recom-

11

mended to Bryce that he also rest in his cabin. The doctor gave it as his opinion that the champagne and orange juice the two men had drunk must have caused their illness.

Meanwhile the storm had grown worse. The *Falconer* was bobbing up and down like a cork on the surface of boiling water and suddenly Dr Forbes had his hands full with a rash of seasickness cases among the other passengers, Candace and Pamela in particular.

When Dr Forbes had time to visit Bryce and Tyler again, both men said they were feeling better. Evelyn, who was still with her husband, asked if the doctor might give Tyler a mild sedative to help him nap. Dr Forbes said it could not hurt and she accompanied the doctor to the ship's galley where he prepared a mixture for her to take to her husband.

Evelyn left the doctor in the galley and was on her way back to her husband's cabin when she encountered Alfred, the butler. Evelyn, explaining to Alfred that she herself was beginning to suffer seasickness, asked him to take the glass to Tyler's cabin. Evelyn went to her own cabin.

Two hours later, when there was a lull in the storm, Evelyn tried to call her husband on the ship's intercom. There was no answer. She tried several more times, there still was no answer, and she went to his cabin. The door was locked — all the cabin doors on the *Falconer* had a deadbolt lock on the inside — and there was no response to her repeated knocks on the door.

She used the intercom in the corridor outside the cabin to call Alfred, instructed him to make a search of the ship for her husband, and then report to her at the door to Tyler's cabin.

She waited there for a long time until Alfred showed up, saying he had been unable to locate Mr Robins.

'All right,' Evelyn said. 'You'll have to get the captain and tell him we have to open the door to this cabin. And Alfred,' she cautioned, 'don't say anything of this to any of the others. No need to spread an alarm yet.'

When Alfred returned, he had Captain Sheffield with him and two of the crewmen who had brought tools with them.

The crewmen had to remove the door from the hinges which were on the outside of the cabin — a job that required the use of pliers, a hammer and chisel, and a crowbar — and then slide the door off the deadbolt lock inside.

Evelyn, Captain Sheffield, the two crewmen, and Alfred stood for a moment in the now-open doorway, taking in the scene in the cabin. At first glance it appeared that everything was in order. Then Evelyn gave a small cry and pointed, and they all saw Tyler Robins's body sprawled out on the floor in front of the desk on the far side of the cabin. Tyler lay on his back, his right side to the doorway.

'Oh!' Evelyn said in a muffled voice and hurried forward. In her haste, she tripped on the hem of the long, flowing kaftan she was wearing and almost lost her balance before she was across the cabin and had flung herself down over her husband's body. The captain, the crewmen, and Alfred stood immobile in the doorway.

There was another cry from Evelyn: 'Oh! Oh! Oh! Someone has stabbed him!' As she moved

13

aside, she lifted Tyler's left shoulder. There was a knife sticking into his side just under the armpit. Evelyn lowered his shoulder gently. 'Get Dr Forbes! Hurry!' she called out, resting on her knees beside the body.

One of the crewmen started to take a step into the cabin and Captain Sheffield motioned the man back, saying, 'I think we should all stay out of the cabin until the doctor gets here.'

Alfred was soon back with Dr Forbes who had brought his black medical bag. Evelyn was still on her knees beside the body. Forbes had to move her aside, saying, 'Let me take a look.'

The doctor tried to take Tyler's pulse with one hand, while removing a stethoscope from his bag with his other hand. The doctor then applied the stethoscope to Tyler's chest, listened for a long time, opened Tyler's closed eyelids, then sank back on his haunches. He looked at Evelyn and shook his head, looked at those standing in the doorway and shook his head again.

'Is he − is he − ?' Evelyn tried to speak in a whispered voice.

'He's gone,' Dr Forbes said.

'Someone killed him,' Evelyn said. She seemed to be in shock.

'Yes, it would seem so.' The doctor nodded his head.

He made a motion to help her to her feet.

'Wait!' Captain Sheffield took a step into the cabin. 'I don't understand. How could someone have killed him? His cabin door was bolted shut from the inside. We had to remove the door from the hinges.' He pointed to the portholes. 'And even though the portholes are large enough for someone to slip through from outside, you can see they are all bolted shut on the inside, too.'

They all took a look around the cabin. As they had noted earlier, everything in it seemed to be in order. The bunk was still made up although the top spread showed a slight depression on it where Tyler had rested when he was feeling ill. On the table beside the bed was a collection of seven or eight books in an orderly stack, the empty glass which had contained the sedative mixture Alfred had brought to the cabin, a box of cigars, an ashtray, and a cigarette lighter. There was a chest of drawers, all of them closed, against one wall and a large steamer trunk at the foot of the bunk.

The only sign of disarray in the cabin was at the desk where Tyler Robins apparently had been sitting just before he died. On the desk top a bottle of ink had overturned and spilled across the desk and dripped onto the floor, and a pen was lying on the floor near the body. The logbook Tyler had been keeping throughout the voyage was open and on the open page were written what must have been his last words: *Wednesday — we have just cr—* and the letters trailed off.

There was, of course, one other article of disorder in the cabin: the knife sticking into Tyler Robins's chest. All of them recognized it as the fishing knife that was usually to be found in the stern of the boat.

Dr Forbes was the one who finally replied to Captain Sheffield's question: 'I don't know the answer to what happened here. That matter will have to wait. For now we must break the news of what's happened here to the others aboard.'

Evelyn agreed and though she was unsteady on

her feet, insisted she would inform her family and asked the captain to tell the other passengers and the crew. Dr Forbes covered the body with a sheet and Captain Sheffield instructed the crewmen to replace the cabin door on its hinges.

Later, those on board the *Falconer* would describe the night that followed as 'a living hell'.

The shock of Tyler Robins's death, the knowledge that there was a murderer on board, would have been enough, but to add to the ordeal, the storm intensified. The wind shrieked, blinding rain flooded down, and huge waves broke over the vessel's deck. The *Falconer* rolled and floundered in the heaving sea. The ship's radio and power went out. The passengers huddled in the flickering light of candles and oil lamps in the saloon, expecting every moment that the *Falconer* would go down.

Gradually, towards morning, the storm passed, leaving grey skies and choppy seas behind. Shaken as they were by the terrifying experience, everyone aboard drew a sigh of relief. Fate, however, had one more surprising twist in store for them.

Captain Sheffield, making the rounds of the ship in the morning to determine the damage the storm might have inflicted, made a new, startling discovery: sometime during the night and the storm, Tyler Robins's body, wrapped in its sheet shroud, had disappeared from his cabin. One of the cabin's portholes stood open. Outside the porthole there was a straight drop into the ocean.

II

Within a few hours of the discovery that Tyler Robins's body was gone from his cabin, power was restored to the *Falconer*. Evelyn immediately used the ship's radio to call the family lawyer, Julian Shields, in New York. She informed the lawyer of the circumstances of her husband's death and the disappearance of the body and asked him to fly to Wake Island so he could meet the *Falconer* when it reached there. She also asked him to bring with him the private investigator who had worked for her husband in the past.

The two men, Julian Shields and private investigator B. J. Grieg, flew out to Wake Island and were waiting there when the *Falconer* completed its limping voyage and finally docked. They went on board before any of the passengers or crew left the ship.

Evelyn then hired Grieg to make a thorough investigation of her husband's death and of what had become of the body, saying, 'Mr Grieg, I don't care how much it costs or how long it takes you, I want you to solve this case.'

The investigator was a stocky man of medium height, in his early forties, and had a hard-edged look, the skin of his face tight across the bones, his eyes cold and unblinking, his clothes looking as if they'd been sewn on him.

The first action Grieg took was to make a complete search of the ship, from stem to stern, top deck to hold. He wanted to make certain that the corpse had not been stowed away secretly somewhere aboard the vessel. The search proved fruitless. Nor could anyone have removed the body at the dockside since they all had obeyed Evelyn's request to stay on the *Falconer* until the investigator had a chance to look the ship over and to question all who had been on the cruise.

Grieg conducted his questioning of the passengers and crew in the ship's main saloon. He spoke with each person alone. He asked the same four questions of each passenger and each member of the crew:

'Did you see or talk to Tyler Robins at any time on the day of his death?'

'Where were you at the time you first heard of his death?'

'Did you enter the cabin of Tyler Robins, for any reason, during the afternoon or evening following his death?'

'Do you know of anyone who might have killed him?'

The investigator planned to continue to ask questions of all those involved, but after this initial interrogation, the passengers and crew were free to leave the *Falconer* and go ashore.

Evelyn had remained silent about the tape recording Tyler had made of his conversation with Paul Bryce. She wanted to wait until other matters were settled before she decided what to do about it. Only Julian Shields knew of the existence of the tape. Before the *Falconer* had reached Wake Island, Evelyn had found both the tape recording and the unfinished letter Tyler had been writing to Cynthia concerning Phillip Wingate.

She had given the letter to Cynthia, who had dismissed her father's written words with an impatient shrug, saying, 'Phillip had already told

18

me about his wife's tragic death. It was an accident. Father was just being overprotective of me. The letter does not change my feelings about dear Phillip.'

The nightmare of Tyler Robins's death did not end for his family with the end of the *Falconer*'s ill-fated voyage.

By the time Evelyn, Marshall, Candace and Cynthia flew back from Wake Island to the family's estate in Maryland, James Robins and his wife, Geneviève, had come over from Paris. Libby and Lewis were there, too, so all the remaining members of the Robins family were together again at Greenlawn.

There were, of course, long family discussions about the murder of Tyler Robins and the strange disappearance of the body. And joining these discussions – at Evelyn's invitation – were Julian Shields and B. J. Grieg.

During these discussions, the lawyer, Shields, usually acted as mediator between the various members of the family, almost all of whom had one theory or another, and between them and the private investigator, who was acknowledged to be the authority on the case.

Julian Shields was well equipped for the role he was called upon to play in these proceedings. He was a man in his late fifties, tall, slim, scholarly-looking, who was, above all, calm, thoughtful, judicious in speech, and sensitive to the feelings of all of them.

During one of the discussions, James Robins exploded in anger at his brother Marshall: 'From all the reports we've heard, everyone on the *Falconer* knew of the tension that existed. You

19

were our father's only son there — why, why, didn't you do something to protect him?'

Marshall's heated reply was: 'I loved Father as much as you did. There was always tension around him, wherever he was. How did I know somebody was going to try to kill him? How could I have known?'

At which point Julian Shields interjected quietly: 'Please! You two must not get into a shouting match. It will only increase the sadness we all suffer from this tragic event.'

The lawyer waited until he felt that the two brothers had had time to think over his words before he added: 'I think it would be more constructive for us to hear what Mr Grieg has to say.'

'Yes,' Evelyn said softly, 'I think you're quite right, Julian.'

All eyes in the room centered on the private investigator as he said he had been able to formulate only one theory to explain how the crime had taken place, based upon his examination of the ship and his not-yet-complete interrogation of those aboard.

'Since we know the cabin was securely locked from the inside, door and portholes, at the time of the discovery of the body, I think the most obvious fact was overlooked. When the cabin door was removed from its hinges, *the murderer must have still been inside somewhere, hiding*! The most likely hiding place would have been in that large steamer trunk at the foot of the bunk.'

'And none of us thought to look there,' Marshall said.

Grieg nodded. 'Exactly! The killer would have

counted on that. In all the excitement of finding Mr Tyler Robins dead, nobody thought of such a thing. Later, after the cabin door was replaced and during all the ensuing confusion, it would have been quite simple for the killer to step out of the trunk and take his or her place among the others.'

Evelyn nodded her head. 'Yes, I can see how that was possible.'

'It seems the most logical explanation,' Grieg said. He paused, then added, 'As to how the body was disposed of later, that would have been a relatively easy matter. Anyone could have slipped into the cabin during the storm, in the darkness with all the power off, and eliminated the body.'

The investigator was silent for a moment, frowning before he said, 'I can only speculate as to the reason why the murderer wanted to dispose of the body. I would imagine because of the fear that some incriminating evidence connected to the body, or perhaps to the murder weapon, the knife, still remained.'

'A question,' Julian Sheilds put in. 'When you spoke with the passengers and crew at the time you first went aboard at Wake Island, could everyone prove where they were at the moment the body was found in the cabin?'

Grieg frowned. 'Everyone *told* me where they were, yes. But not everyone could prove that what they told me was true. In other words, they had no witnesses to back up what they were saying — to corroborate their precise whereabouts at that particular time.'

'And how many such persons were there?' Shields asked.

'Oh, three or four of the passengers,' the investi-

21

gator replied, 'and perhaps half the crew.'

'So,' Shields said, 'presumably one of these is the murderer?'

Grieg nodded slowly. 'Yes, assuming my theory is correct.' He raised a cautioning hand. 'However, the fact that either a passenger or a crew member was unable to produce a witness as to where he or she was, does not necessarily make them a prime suspect. Let me give you an example.'

He paused before he went on, 'Take the case of Mr Phillip Wingate, for instance. He was one of the last to learn of the death of Mr Robins. That's because he was not in his cabin at the time Mrs Robins here went about informing the passengers of the tragedy. However, he says he had gone to Janice Elgar's cabin at the time to speak to her. She wasn't there and he says he waited. Now, at that time Miss Elgar *wasn't* in her cabin. She was with Miss Candace Robins in another cabin. So, in a way, Miss Elgar's statement negatively supports Mr Wingate's.'

The investigator concluded his remarks by saying that he planned to continue his questioning of everyone who had been on the *Falconer*.

A few days after the family discussions at Greenlawn, the U.S. Coast Guard — which had jurisdiction over crimes committed aboard all vessels of American registry — conducted an inquiry into the murder of Tyler Robins. Since the *Falconer*'s home port was Wilmington, the inquiry took place in Philadelphia. After hearing testimony and considering all the available evidence, the Board of Inquiry concluded: 'Tyler Robins met his death at the hands of a person or persons unknown. . . .'

22

NOTES

NOTES

CHAPTER TWO

I

During the weeks after the Coast Guard inquiry into the death of Tyler Robins, James became obsessed with the need to discover the identity of his father's murderer and began to devise a plan to unmask the killer.

He knew the circumstances had to be right, however, and so he was forced to bide his time.

Meanwhile, there were other events taking place in the affairs of the family. There was, for instance, the matter of the reading of Tyler Robins's will in the offices of Julian Shields in Manhattan.

It was a sombre yet suspenseful moment, sombre because of the death and suspenseful because every member of the family knew how unpredictable Tyler Robins had always been. They were all there: Evelyn in her widow's weeds — with John Forbes at her side for moral support — Marshall, James, Lewis, Libby, Candace and Cynthia, not one of them knowing what surprises Tyler might have in store for them.

As it turned out, there were no surprises. According to the will, Tyler left his estate, including Robins Cosmetics, in seven equal shares to his wife and six children.

In the will, he specified that since he had not yet decided upon a successor to replace him as head of the company, his wife, Evelyn, be empowered to run the business for one year, with the help of all six of the children, of course. At the end of one year, during which each of them would have time to decide who among them was best qualified to run Robins Cosmetics, the seven of them would vote for a new president and chairman of the board.

If any of them in the room were disappointed not to have been handed the reins of the company, they managed to conceal their feelings. Nor did anyone remark on Marshall's great good luck that Tyler had not cut him out of the will, as had been threatened. And while Evelyn's initial reaction was one of incredulity at finding herself the head of the business, she quickly recovered and gave every appearance of being capable of the task.

Several days later a memorial service was conducted for Tyler Robins. George Pittman, Libby's husband, had taken charge of the service. He had designed and had had constructed a huge marble monument to Tyler. On the day the service took place, the monument was unveiled in the Robins family plot at a small cemetery in the Green Spring Valley of Maryland, not far from the family estate. There was a large turnout of Tyler's friends, acquaintances and business associates for the ceremony. Afterwards, most of those attending were invited back to the house at the Greenlawn estate.

Throughout all the events of the past weeks

James Robins had been plotting out a plan to uncover the identity of his father's murderer. Now, he decided, the time had come to try it out since all of those who had been on the cruise — one of whom had killed his father — were present in one place. Not only had all the passengers who had been aboard the *Falconer* attended the memorial service but Captain Ian Sheffield and the yacht's entire crew, as well, had come to Maryland to pay their respects.

To make his plan work, James needed all the passengers, the captain, Sheffield, and two of the crewmen — the yacht's cook, Arturo, and the steward, Percival — who had had words with Tyler before his death. James had, by that time, already evolved his own theory as to who the killer was but the trick was to make him show his hand.

It was with this in mind that James, towards the end of the day, managed to assemble in the library all those who he felt could reasonably be considered suspects in the murder. To get them into one room together, he used the pretext of telling them he wanted to speak a few words in memory of his father.

The Robins library was a vast, cathedral-like room, three of its sides lined by glass-fronted bookcases extending from floor to ceiling. There were two windows in the fourth wall and, between the windows, another glass-fronted case which contained Tyler Robins's collection of guns: rifles, shotguns, handguns, an ancient musket. The remainder of this wall was covered by framed prints of hunting scenes. The floor of the library was covered in deep carpeting from wall to wall. In the centre of the room was an enormous, round, oak table, surrounded by leather armchairs. More leather armchairs were set back against the bookcases. A crystal chandelier hung down from the ceiling directly over the table. Tyler Robins had had the library designed and constructed so it could serve as a conference room when he held business meetings at Greenlawn.

Once everyone was in the library, James let them wander around the room and asked Alfred to take drink orders, to put them at ease before he revealed the real reason for bringing them all together.

Finally, when everyone had been served, they took places around the table at James's suggestion, James standing with his hands on the back of the chair he had selected for himself. It was dark outside now and the room's light came from the chandelier above the table.

'I thank all of you for joining me here,' James said, still standing. 'As I told you, I have a few words I'd like to say in memory of my father.'

He paused, a faint smile on his lips, turned away from the table, and walked over to the glass-fronted gun case against the wall. He opened the case and took out a revolver, turning his head toward the table as he said, 'My father kept his guns here, all well-oiled, all loaded, as I've checked to make certain myself these past days.'

He closed the case and, carrying the revolver, returned to the table. He sat down in the chair he'd selected for himself and, his movements very deliberate, placed the gun on the table in front of him.

'Actually' — the faint smile was on his lips again

28

— 'when I told you I have a few words I'd like to say in memory of my father, I should more correctly have said, in memory of my father's murder. Because that's what we're going to talk about now.' He leaned forward and patted the revolver lying on the table. 'And I intend to get the answer right now.'

There was a stir in the room and several exclamations of protest.

James paused and looked from one face to another of those sitting around the table and — because there was not enough space to accommodate all the chairs at the table — to the faces of those who had had to pull up chairs and were sitting just behind those around the table.

Next to him was his mother, Evelyn. Julian Shields had pulled a chair up behind her. Next to her sat Dr John Forbes. The twins, Cynthia and Candace, were in the next two chairs, with Phillip Wingate beside them. Wingate had brought his sister, Ava, from England with him, and she sat in a pulled-up chair just behind him. Continuing on around the table were seated Marshall, Janice Elgar, Pamela Robins — she and Marshall were still estranged — Paul Bryce, Alfred, and Captain Ian Sheffield. The yacht's two crewmen, Arturo and Percival, sat in chairs behind the captain. The private investigator, B. J. Grieg, was in the room also but had taken a chair that remained back against the bookcases, as if to separate himself from the proceedings — which in fact he had disapproved of when James had confided them to him beforehand. James had not invited his other brother and sister, Lewis and Libby, although both were present at Greenlawn.

29

James had also told his plan beforehand to his mother and Julian Shields — both of whom fruitlessly tried to talk him out of going through with it — and to the butler, Alfred, and Alfred's wife, Dorina, whose help he needed.

James thought the plan was simplicity itself: someone in this room had killed his father. In a moment James would announce that he was going to name the murderer. As soon as he made the statement, Alfred would surreptitiously press a button under the table, which would sound a buzzer in the kitchen and signal Dorina, standing by the fuse box there, to cut off the lights in the library. The revolver which James had taken from the gun case and which now lay on the table in front of him actually contained blanks. James believed that when the lights went out, the guilty party — thinking he or she was about to be revealed — would snatch up the revolver and fire at him (James had positioned himself in front of a window so there would be a clear silhouette of him). The guilty party would not know, of course, that the shot would be harmless. Then, the moment the revolver was fired, Alfred would again signal Dorina who would restore the lights in the library. Tyler Robins's murderer — and the would-be murderer of James himself — would be caught redhanded holding the gun.

James looked slowly around the table once more and said, 'I am now going to announce the name of my father's murderer, who is in this room right now, and show you proof of who the killer is.'

James saw Alfred reach under the table where the signal button was located and, in the next moment, the lights went out, leaving the room in total darkness except for the faint illumination that marked the windows.

There was immediate confusion in the darkness of the room. Several voices cried out in alarm and there was the sound of a chair overturning here and there.

James, who had been prepared, had leaned forward in his chair in the darkness, resting the tips of his fingers against the bottom of the handgrip of the revolver lying on the table. For several moments nothing happened. Then, to his delight, James felt the gun being slowly pulled away from him across the table.

More time went by — in the darkness it seemed longer than it probably was — and a shot rang out. There was more confusion and shouting in the room, in the darkness, and suddenly the lights came on again, dazzling in their brightness. There were more shouts, more confusion. James lay sprawled sideways in his chair, a bullet hole in the centre of his head.

Dr John Forbes rushed to James, felt for his pulse, and finally shook his head sadly.

'James! He's dead!' The strangled cry came from Evelyn.

'Look! Look!' Paul Bryce shouted, pointing to the side of the table opposite James. 'The butler! The butler, he did it!'

All eyes turned from James to look in the direction Bryce was pointing.

Alfred Wales stood at the table between two chairs. He was holding by the barrel the revolver that had been lying on the table.

'No! No! You've got it all wrong!' Alfred protested, taking a couple of steps backwards.

'*He did it!*' Bryce insisted. 'He has the gun in his hand.'

The butler looked around the table. 'You have it all wrong,' he said, shaking his head. 'In the darkness, after the lights went out, my hand was on the table. Someone pushed the gun at me. I thought it was Mr James. I picked up the gun. I had it in my hands but I didn't fire it. The shot came from another gun in the room.'

At that point several people started for the door.

'Stop!' Julian Shields called out quickly. 'Nobody is to leave the room.' Shields looked at B. J. Grieg. 'Mr Grieg,' he said to the private investigator, 'Guard the door.'

Grieg moved quickly, putting his back to the closed door.

Shields pointed and said, 'Marshall, call the police. Tell them what's happened and to come at once.'

Marshall hurried to the phone which sat on a small table near the window.

The lawyer came around the table and approached Alfred. 'Now, let's see what this is all about. If that is the gun that James placed on the table, it shouldn't have been able to kill him even if it was fired. Alfred, give the gun to Mr Grieg and let him check it.'

Alfred walked across the room wordlessly and handed the gun to the private investigator who broke open the chamber.

'There's only one unfired shell in here,' Grieg said flatly. He held the end of the revolver's barrel to his nose and added, 'This gun hasn't been fired. It was another gun that killed James Robins.'

'The police are on the way,' Marshall said

loudly, hanging up the phone. 'They said not to touch anything in the room until they arrived.'

'I suggest,' Julian Shields said, 'that we all take our seats and remain calm.'

Overturned chairs were righted and everyone, except Grieg who still stood at the door, sat down around the table again. It was only then that they discovered one of the chairs was empty, the chair where the yacht's steward, Percival, had been sitting. He was not in the library. There was no place in the room where he could hide.

'He had to have slipped out the door,' Shields said, 'probably in all the confusion just after the shot was fired.'

Grieg spoke up: 'Then he'll be long gone from these parts by now. We'll just have to let the police catch him.'

They were all silent, except for Evelyn's soft weeping, until finally the police came, pounding on the library door. Grieg moved aside to let them enter.

There were three police officers, two of them in state-trooper uniforms, the third a huge man in plain clothes who turned out to be a state-police homicide sergeant named Horgan. He was in charge.

Grieg identified himself to Sergeant Horgan as a private investigator and gave him a detailed explanation of the events that had occurred.

Horgan nodded his head, went to the phone, called the state police barracks, put out an arrest bulletin on Percival — based upon Grieg's description of the missing yacht's steward — and asked that more police units be despatched to the estate.

That done, Sergeant Horgan instructed one of the troopers to search everyone in the room for the missing gun. He directed the other trooper to check through the house and determine whether anyone in the other rooms had seen the ship's steward, Percival, leave the house.

The sergeant, meanwhile, wandered around the room. He examined the bookcases, the gun case — which he found unlocked and with a second gun gone — and even got down on his hands and knees and crawled under the table. It was from this spot that he suddenly loudly exclaimed, 'Ah — ha! What have we here? I think we've found the weapon we want.'

Horgan backed out from under the table, leaving the weapon untouched, but with the beam of his flashlight shining on it. Those in the room who were curious enough bent down and peered beneath the table where they could see the small black automatic lying on the thick carpeting. The spot where it lay was almost dead centre under the table.

The trooper finished his search of the people in the room. No other gun was found. The second trooper returned to report he could find no one in the other parts of the house who had observed Percival leaving.

A short time later the additional police units requested by Sergeant Horgan arrived. These included the medical examiner and members of the forensic unit who would collect whatever evidence they could find for later scientific analysis.

The gun was retrieved from under the table. It proved to have been fired, and later ballistics tests confirmed that it was the murder weapon. The gun had been wiped clean of any fingerprints, and anyone in the room could have tossed it under the table. Questioning by Sergeant Horgan revealed that during the period of darkness in the room before the shot was fired, there had been enough time for anyone to cross to the gun case and remove the automatic.

The police photographer shot dozens of pictures of James slumped in his chair as well as photographs of all the people in the room sitting or standing in the exact locations where they claimed that they'd been when the fatal shot was fired.

Other troopers were sent to make a search of the house for the ship's steward who had skipped out.

The police spent the next few hours taking statements from all those who had been present at the time of the shooting. Dorina, Alfred's wife, was also brought in to give a statement on the part she had played in turning off the library lights. The housekeeper had been upstairs in the quarters she and Alfred shared when the police located her and asked her to come to the library.

She was wearing a housecoat, said she had been washing her hair, and appeared bewildered at the scene in the library. She said she had known nothing of the shooting until then, had simply switched the lights off and on at the signal from her husband, as James Robins had instructed her to do.

When the troopers who had been searching the house for the missing man, Percival, returned, they reported that they had been unable to find any trace of him.

Daylight was just dawning when the police

concluded their work at the estate, taking the body of James with them when they left.

Later that same morning the Robins's gardener spotted a body floating in the swimming pool.

The police were again called and, when they arrived, fished the corpse out of the water. The dead man was identified as Percival, who had disappeared the night before. There were no signs or marks of violence on the body to suggest foul play. The police could only surmise that the ship's steward, in trying to flee the murder scene and the estate — perhaps in panicked guilt — had accidentally fallen into the pool and drowned.

II

There would, of course, have to be autopsies performed on the bodies of both James and Percival. While they awaited the results, the police carried on an intensive investigation of all those who had been present in the library at the time James had been fatally shot. In addition, the police requested, and received, permission to examine James's room and the articles he had left behind in the house.

One result of this search was that homicide sergeant Horgan came across a curious letter which was hidden away in the bottom of a steamer trunk James had brought with him from Paris. There was no postmark on the outside of the envelope, just the name: Mr James Robins.

The letter, on a single sheet of white stationery, was typewritten:

YOU THINK YOU ARE VERY CLEVER AND THAT NO
ONE KNOWS WHAT YOU ARE UP TO. BUT YOU'RE
WRONG. I KNOW. GIVE UP YOUR PLAN. YOU'RE
NOT GOING TO CATCH ME. I HAVE TOO MUCH TO
LOSE. I WILL KILL YOU. YOU ARE WARNED.

Since there was no postmark on the envelope,
the police had to assume that the letter had been
left somewhere for James to find. They were aware
that he could have received the letter in Paris and
brought it with him. But it seemed more likely that
it had reached him while he was at Greenlawn.

Yet when Sergeant Horgan questioned those
people James might have been expected to tell
about the letter, all denied ever having heard of it
from him.

James's wife, Geneviève, could only shake her
head and say no, no, he had not spoken of it to her.
Nor did she know it was hidden away in the
trunk.

Evelyn said: 'He told me about his plan, as he
did others, but he never mentioned receiving such
a letter. If he had, I would have tried even harder
to talk him out of going through with his charade
in the library.'

B. J. Grieg had an explanation for the police of
why he thought James wouldn't have told anyone
about the letter: 'Those of us who knew what he
planned to do were all against it and attempted to
persuade him not to do it. Certainly if we, or at
least if I, had learned about such a letter, he would
not have been allowed to stage his little scene. And
I think that's why he didn't tell anyone.'

'Yes, I can understand that,' Horgan said. And
then he said grimly: 'Whoever wrote that letter

must have been the murderer of Tyler Robins, and must have found out somehow what James was going to try to pull off.'

The sergeant sent the letter to the police laboratory to be analysed but he had no real conviction that it would reveal any clues as to who had written it.

Later, when Julian Shields and Evelyn were alone, the lawyer said thoughtfully: 'There was one particular sentence in that letter to James that struck me as possibly significant. The sentence "I have too much to lose." Only you and I know about that tape recording Tyler made of his talk with Paul Bryce. Those words sound like something Bryce might write.'

'I suppose so,' Evelyn said, frowning. 'But then, couldn't that be true of almost anyone, assuming they were about to be unmasked as Tyler's killer?'

'Yes, yes,' Julian answered. 'Still . . .' He let his words and the suggestion trail off there.

At another point in the investigation, Sergeant Horgan wanted to re-enact the scene in the library at the time James was shot. He asked those who had been there to once again take the seats where they'd sat on the previous occasion.

Reluctantly, they all filed into the room: Evelyn, Julian, Dr Forbes, Cynthia and Candace, Phillip Wingate and his sister, Ava, Marshall and the wife from whom he was separated, Pamela, Janice Elgar, Paul Bryce, Captain Ian Sheffield, Alfred, and the yacht's cook, Arturo. They took seats, one chair — where the dead Percival had sat — remaining empty. B. J. Grieg again took up his position at the rear of the room. Lewis Robins, who had not been present either on the yacht or in the library, looked on curiously from the open doorway. Sergeant Horgan himself had taken the chair where James had been sitting.

It was clear to all of them in the room that they were a group ill at ease. The only one who actually seemed to be unable to go through the re-enactment was Phillip Wingate's sister, Ava. Almost as soon as she sat down, she rose, trembling, to say in a shaky voice, 'I'm − I'm − so − sorry. But I feel quite faint.'

Lewis, standing at the doorway, immediately rushed to her side, protesting, 'Look here, Sergeant, surely you can spare Miss Wingate this ordeal. Particularly since she would not possibly be a suspect in my father's death as she wasn't even on the yacht.'

'It's true she isn't a suspect,' the sergeant answered. 'It's just that I had hoped everyone who was here in the library might now be able to recall exactly what he or she saw and heard when the lights went out and the shot was fired.'

'Yes, yes, I understand that,' Lewis said brusquely. 'Nevertheless, I would think you could make an exception to Miss Wingate when you can clearly see how distressed she is.'

'All right. All right.' Horgan waved a hand in the air. 'Miss Wingate, you're excused.'

Lewis then led the young woman from the room, she leaning gratefully on his arm.

The re-enactment continued, with various people supplying such facts as they could recall.

Evelyn said: 'In the instance the room went dark, I could hear sounds of people moving around. But it was all so unreal, so shapeless that I really can't tell you anything that would be of help to you.'

Julian Shields stated: 'Because James had told me what he planned to do, I wasn't caught by surprise when the lights went out and the shot was fired. Believing the shot was a blank, why, it just never occurred to me to be particularly observant. My whole attention was directed to the moment when the lights would go on and I would be able to see who was holding the gun with the blank cartridge.'

B. J. Grieg, who had also known of the plan in advance, said much the same thing as Julian. And so did Alfred, except that he did add: 'Holding the gun with the blank cartridge, as I was, my greatest shock came when the other gun was fired. I was so shocked in fact that it took me several moments to collect my wits and press the buzzer to signal my wife to turn on the lights again.'

The other observations offered to the sergeant were generally vague as to who moved where or did what while the room was in darkness. The one seemingly positive fact to emerge from the group assembled was an explanation of how Percival had managed to slip out of the room unobserved. Everyone agreed that when the lights in the room came up again, after the shooting, all attention — including B. J. Grieg's — had been focused on James Robins slumped in his chair. Thus it had been easy for Percival to leave without being noticed.

A day after Sergeant Horgan had had everyone gather in the library, the police investigation into Percival's background turned up another piece of evidence: the ship's steward had a record of past violence. There were arrests, which he had concealed when he signed on the *Falconer*, for assault and assault with a deadly weapon, and a fugitive warrant for manslaughter outstanding on him in the state of Mississippi.

The police speculated that while these heretofore unknown facts about him could explain why he panicked and ran — knowing the police would arrive and, eventually, his past would be revealed — his record also marked him as a person capable of violent behaviour who might kill under certain circumstances.

Of those days during the police investigation, Evelyn would write in her diary:

How difficult everything has become, with the police under foot all the time and asking questions of everyone! And everyone so suspicious of everyone else! One hardly knows what to think. And it was so foolish for James to try to stage that stunt of his. Mr Grieg suggested to the family the other night that Tyler's murder and James's murder might not be connected at all — that is, that James might not have beer killed by the same person who killed Tyler. When John Forbes asked Mr Grieg what he meant, Mr Grieg said that perhaps someone in the library who had nothing to do with killing Tyler might nevertheless be fearful that James intended naming him and — because this person had something else to hide, and it might come out if he was named — killed James before he could speak.

In another entry in the diary Evelyn would write:

41

Though we all mourn James, I have come to the realization that I must also attend to the needs of the living — not only to the needs of his widow, Geneviève, but also to the needs of poor Carrie and her child, Molly, James's daughter and my grandchild. I have had to make a hard, lonely decision: whether to tell Geneviève of this situation or not. Rightly or wrongly, I have concluded that no useful purpose would be served in telling her, so I intend to say nothing. I did, however, make arrangements so that neither Carrie nor Molly will ever have to worry about money for as long as they live. I'm sure this is what James would have wanted and would have done himself if he had lived. When I told Carrie and her parents, Alfred and Dorina, what I had done, they were so grateful that I was deeply touched. Anyhow, I'm glad to have that behind me. Now, if only the police would complete their investigation and we could get it behind us . .

In subsequent days, the autopsies on James's body and Percival's body were completed. The autopsies confirmed that Percival's death had been caused by drowning, and that James Robins had died as the result of a bullet wound in the head.

Within the same week, a coroner's inquest was held into the shooting of James Robins. As had been the case in the earlier murder of Tyler Robins, there were many suspects but no conclusive proof pointing to the killer. It was clear from the testimony that the majority — but not all — of those who had been present suspected that the ship's steward, Percival, was the guilty party. If he had not drowned, he would probably have been indicted, though he might not have been found guilty had he stood trial, because of the lack of any solid evidence. In any event, Percival was not there to testify and it was because of the lack of sure evidence that the verdict of the coroner's inquest was: 'James Robins met his death at the hands of a person or persons unknown. . . .'

James was buried in the family plot in the cemetery where the monument to his father stood. George Pittman again designed and had constructed the tombstone under which the body was buried.

NOTES

NOTES

CHAPTER THREE

I

Cynthia Robins had ignored her father's warnings about Phillip Wingate, contained in the unfinished letter Tyler had been writing before he died, and she was determined to marry the Englishman.

After a proper period of waiting following the deaths of her father and brother, she and Wingate were married at his English home, Meadlands. All the remaining members of the Robins family were present. Candace was the bridesmaid; Marshall, as the eldest son, gave away the bride, and Phillip Wingate chose Lewis Robins to be his best man. Phillip and Lewis had become good friends during the first occasion they'd been together, at Greenlawn when the memorial service was being held for Tyler Robins and James had been fatally shot. In addition, Lewis had become quite smitten with Phillip's sister, Ava, in the time they'd been together in Maryland.

Following the wedding, Cynthia had come up with a rather original idea for her honeymoon with Phillip Wingate. She had learned from the news that the *Orient Express*, the legendary train, was running again across France, Switzerland, and Italy to Venice. Many well-to-do people were making the trip a holiday in itself.

Cynthia had planned that most of her family who had been at the wedding, along with Ava, Phillip's sister, would travel with her and Phillip. The others would make it a round trip journey while she and her new husband would leave them in Venice and continue on their honeymoon.

Because they had to return home to New Jersey, Libby and George Pittman were the only members of the family to drop out.

The rest of them decided to go along: Evelyn, Marshall, Candace and Lewis, as well as Ava. Both Dr John Forbes and Julian Shields, who had attended the wedding and been invited on the train trip, had also accepted.

To begin the journey from England, the party boarded the train, now known as the Venice *Simplon-Orient-Express*, at Victoria Station. Almost immediately the group assembled in the Pullman dining car, *Cygnus*, to make the run to Folkestone. They ate while travelling through the greenery of the Kent countryside.

At Folkestone, the group boarded the Sealink ferry for the ninety-minute Channel crossing — past the White Cliffs of Dover — to Boulogne. There they went through Customs and Immigration and momentarily separated into their various compartments in the 1920s' *Compagnie Internationale des Wagons-Lits et des Grands Express Européens* sleeper.

As soon as they had checked out their accommodations in the comfortable compartments, all the members of the wedding party met for drinks in the *bar-salon* car where they would spend most of their time together when they were not dining in the elegant restaurant car.

The newly-weds, Cynthia and Phillip, sat together at one table, with Ava and Lewis. Marshall and his sister Candace sat at the next table, and across the aisle were Evelyn, Julian Shields and John Forbes. It did not escape the attention of the members of the group that Dr Forbes appeared out of sorts with Evelyn and Julian, who had not been far apart from one another since the trip had begun.

Evelyn seemed to be making an effort to be cheerful and joking as they sipped champagne. Later, however, after the *Orient Express* had passed over the River Seine and pulled into the Gare d'Austerlitz in Paris, Evelyn, who had been gazing out the window, gave a small cry. She had been idly watching baggage being loaded onto the train and new passengers boarding. Her eye had been caught by the sight of a huge wooden crate, somewhat resembling a coffin, which had been placed in the baggage car. And then as she turned her head away, she had one brief glimpse of a figure outside the window, mounting the steps to one of the *wagon-lits* ahead.

It was the sight of this figure that caused her to exclaim aloud: 'Why that was Paul Bryce! Whatever in the world is he doing getting on this train here in Paris?'

'Paul Bryce?' Julian asked. 'Are you sure?'

Evelyn nodded. 'Yes. Or at least I think I am. Go see. Hurry! I think it was the fourth car ahead.'

John Forbes was frowning. 'Paul Bryce? Why would he be on this train?'

Julian was standing. 'I'm sure it couldn't have been Bryce. But I'll check and see.'

John stood abruptly. 'I'll go with you.'

As the two men left the car, Candace, sitting with Marshall and also watching out the window, received a surprise of her own and also exclaimed aloud: 'Oh, no, no, no, no!'

Marshall, startled by his sister's distressed voice, asked, 'What is it, Candace?'

'That man who just passed by my window and boarded the train,' Candace said. 'He's Steven Boland, one of my ex-boyfriends in London. Oh, I thought he would finally leave me alone. And now he's on this very train. Marshall, I'm scared!'

Marshall covered Candace's hand with one of his own. 'Why are you so frightened?'

Candace hesitated for a moment before she answered, leaning across the table and keeping her voice low so the others in the *bar-salon* wouldn't hear.

'I broke off with Steven some time ago,' she said. 'He worked as an accountant in our London office where I met him. We dated for a while but then I didn't like his possessive manner and I told him I didn't want to date him any longer.'

She paused, trembling, before she continued: 'He quit his job and I thought, Good! I wouldn't have to see him ever again. But then he began writing me notes, threatening notes, and I received phone calls from him, threatening phone calls, all saying that if I didn't start dating him again something terrible would happen to me!'

'And you didn't tell anyone about this?' Marshall asked. 'Try to have him stopped?'

Candace shook her head. 'Not at first. I didn't want to cause a scandal. But then I discovered he was following me everywhere I went. I was scared enough when that happened to tell Father. Father said he'd handle the matter, not to tell anyone else, and I guess he did. I didn't see or hear from Steven again — until now. And here he is on the same train.'

'It could be a coincidence,' Marshall said.

'No. No.' Candace was shaking her head. 'He probably read in one of the London society columns that we were taking this trip and he deliberately came to Paris to board the train. And he means to harm me. He once said in one of his threatening phone calls that if he couldn't have me, he'd kill me.'

'Well, he won't get the chance,' Marshall said firmly. 'Whenever you're out of my sight, I'll always keep a close eye on him. Don't worry.'

The train was off again, gathering speed as it moved out of the Paris station.

Cynthia and her bridegroom, and Lewis and Ava, sitting together, were oblivious to the distress being experienced by both Candace and Evelyn.

Evelyn had finished her glass of champagne and poured herself another before Julian Shields and John Forbes returned from their search through the sleeping cars ahead.

Julian was shaking his head as he and John rejoined Evelyn at the table. 'No luck, I'm afraid,' he said. 'We went through all the cars but couldn't catch sight of anyone even resembling Paul Bryce.'

'But you couldn't have looked in every compartment,' Evelyn said.

Julian patted her hand. 'No, my dear, of course not. Where the compartment doors were closed, we couldn't very well open them and barge in, now could we?'

50

Evelyn sighed. 'I suppose not. And he could be hiding behind any one of them.'

'If he is,' John Forbes said, 'he'll have to surface sometime. If, of course, it actually was Bryce.'

Evelyn was not satisfied but she said nothing more. What worried her was that after she had taken over Robins Cosmetics she had had a secret meeting with Paul Bryce. At the meeting, she had played a copy of the tape recording Tyler had made of his conversation with Bryce. Evelyn had then made it clear to him that she expected him to pay the five million dollars Tyler had demanded. Bryce, having no other choice except to be hauled into court, had agreed but had asked for one month in which to raise the money. The month would be up in ten days, by which time Evelyn would have returned to New York City. And now, she was convinced, Paul Bryce was here on the train, with God knows what plan in mind.

A short time later Candace, at another table, glanced up and then gripped Marshall's hand as she saw Steven Boland enter the *bar-salon*.

She could scarcely believe Boland's audacity when he walked straight up to the table where she and Marshall were sitting.

'Miss Robins,' Boland said, making a mock bow toward her. 'Fancy meeting you here. What a small world it is.'

Candace had shrunk back in her chair but Marshall had jumped to his feet, saying, 'Now look here, you, stay away from my sister. She wants nothing to do with you. Do you understand me? Now clear out.'

Boland eyed Marshall coolly before he answered. 'Ah yes, the big brother. Marshall, isn't it? Well,

Mr Marshall Robins, I have news for you: this is a public train and I have as much right to come and go on it as I please.'

'You've come,' Marshall said in a tight voice, 'now do yourself a favour and please go.'

'Exactly my thought,' Boland said, moving away and taking a seat alone at a table next to the one where Lewis and Ava sat with Cynthia and Phillip. Steven Boland was a sandy-haired, chunky young man not over thirty years old.

It was at this point that there arrived in the *bar-salon* a couple who were so striking in appearance that they caught the eye of everyone present.

'Why, I know them!' John Forbes exclaimed, rising and hurrying towards the elderly man and young woman who had just come in.

He spoke with the two briefly, then brought them over to introduce them.

The man, John Forbes explained, was Joachim, a magician of extraordinary ability, and the young woman, a lovely Eurasian named Genet, was his assistant. John Forbes had seen Joachim performing in a nightclub in Paris the previous year and had been impressed by his magic skills.

The magician was tall, appeared to be quite old, and had a great flowing mane of white hair and dark brooding eyes set in deep sockets in an impassive face that looked as if it were carved out of mahogany. He had also been deaf since birth which made his abilities even more remarkable. He communicated by sign language with the young woman, Genet, who then explained what he was saying.

When John Forbes asked what they were doing on the train, Joachim's fingers spelled out the answer while Genet spoke it aloud:

'Joachim say we just finished engagement in Paris and now we go to Naples for a rest.'

At the coaxing of John Forbes, the two sat for a while, had a pot of tea, and then bade the others a good day and went back to their separate compartments.

After they had departed, Cynthia whispered to Marshall, 'I wish that magician could make Steven Boland disappear.'

The *Orient Express* continued its journey throughout the rest of the day and early morning but there was a definite pall hanging over Evelyn and Candace.

Later in the evening Lewis had left Ava briefly, and while he was gone, Steven Boland attempted to strike up a conversation with Ava. When Lewis returned, Boland left the *bar-salon* for the night. Cynthia and Phillip had already retired to their compartment and Evelyn, John Forbes and Julian Shields departed soon after for their separate quarters.

It was then that Marshall and Candace joined Lewis and Ava for a nightcap and Candace told the latter two her story about Steven Boland.

When she had finished, Ava exclaimed, 'What a terrible man he must be! He was a stranger to me. We exchanged only chit-chat just now. But certainly I shall not acknowledge him again.'

Not long afterwards, the four of them also went to their separate compartments, Marshall making sure Candace was locked in before he left her.

Marshall did not sleep well that night, despite the luxurious comforts of the train, and was relieved next morning — when they all began to assemble again in one of the restaurant cars — at the sight of his sister Candace, looking rested and refreshed. Marshall hadn't really believed that Steven Boland would attempt to attack her during the night. But now that they were all together again, and Boland as well at another table in the restaurant car, Marshall redoubled his resolve not to let Steven Boland out of his sight if Candace was not there.

For the moment at least, Marshall was pleased to see, he would not have to worry about Steven Boland because that young man finished his breakfast and left the restaurant car.

By that time in the journey, the train was in Switzerland, threading its way through the Rhône Valley vineyards. Evelyn, John Forbes and Julian Shields were at one table in the restaurant car, Cynthia, Phillip, Lewis and Ava at another, and Marshall and Candace at a third.

They all dawdled over breakfast except for the bride, Cynthia, who said she was going back to the compartment to freshen up.

Soon after that, Marshall, too, left the restaurant car after first exacting a promise from Candace that she would remain close to the others until he returned.

Quite a time passed before Phillip remarked to the others that Cynthia seemed to be taking a long while. Julian Shields said he would go and get her while those still at the tables — Evelyn, John Forbes, Candace, Phillip, Lewis and Ava — decided to move to the *bar-salon*.

They were all there, sitting at tables, when Julian and one of the *wagon-lit* conductors came rushing into the car.

Julian's face was grave when he announced, 'I'm afraid there's been a terrible accident. A tragedy! It's — Cynthia — '

'Cynthia?' Phillip asked, rising. 'What's happened to her?'

'She's — ' Julian could not go on and raised a futile hand in the air and let it drop.

'I want to see her,' Dr John Forbes said. He stood and followed Julian and the conductor from the *bar-salon*, all the others in the group close behind them.

The door to Cynthia and Phillip's compartment was closed. When the conductor opened the door, Julian stepped aside and John entered, the others crowding into the open doorway.

The doctor's body hid Cynthia from the view of the rest of them. They could see only that she lay on the still opened-out double berth. Then John Forbes turned and said softly, 'She's dead.'

'Dead?' Phillip Wingate shouted. 'I want to see.' The voices of the others could be heard saying the same thing.

'It's not a pretty sight,' John Forbes said, but when the others demanded to see, he shrugged and moved aside.

Cynthia Wingate lay on her back on the berth. She was completely dressed. Her eyes were open and staring. At first glance it was difficult to make out what had happened to her: the lights were off in the compartment and, outside, the train was temporarily in shadow before passing into sunlight again.

Then those peering in through the doorway saw that a strand of steel wire was wrapped, in a curious and awkward fashion, around the lower part of her face — just under the chin — and the back of her neck. (Later it would be speculated that she must have jerked her head up and down or backwards and forwards when her attacker attempted to garrotte her and so he had made a clumsy job of it.) Nevertheless, the killer had been successful enough so that a part of the steel wire had been cruelly embedded in the upper flesh of her throat.

'She's been strangled,' John Forbes said softly — an unnecessary remark but he seemed to need to say something.

Evelyn and Phillip had to be helped away from the scene. All of them looked in shock. Marshall was grim and white-lipped when he was found in his compartment and told the news.

There were, of course, certain procedures to be followed on the train in extraordinary circumstances such as this. The *wagon-lit* conductor had already notified the *chef du train*, who was in charge aboard the *Orient Express*. He, in turn, had a lock put on the compartment where the murder had been committed, and a guard posted at the door. Since it was impossible to determine the exact moment when Cynthia had been killed — and the train had crossed from Switzerland to Italy between the time she had left the restaurant car and the time her body had been found — it would not be possible to decide which country had jurisdiction over the investigation. Therefore, the decision was made that the train would continue on non-stop to its terminal point in Venice.

At Julian Shields's suggestion, the *chef du train* did go through the line of cars, questioning the passengers. None of them had anything to reveal or, if they did, would not say. Julian accompanied the *chef du train* through the coaches and did discover one thing: Evelyn had been right in believing that Paul Bryce was aboard, in one of the compartments behind a closed door.

When Bryce saw Julian, he explained that he had booked onto the *Orient Express* because he knew Evelyn would be on the train. Bryce's further explanation was that he had stayed in his compartment because he didn't want to intrude upon the wedding party which he had known was aboard, information he claimed to have read in the newspapers. He had planned, he said, to appear on the return trip from Venice when he hoped he would have a chance to talk with Evelyn.

Julian and Paul Bryce returned together to the *bar-salon* where most of the group who were with the wedding party had got together again. Candace was the only one who was absent, saying she needed to be alone in her compartment. Marshall did not follow her since Steven Boland was also in the bar car and Marshall could keep an eye on him there. Paul Bryce went back to his compartment.

The magician, Joachim, and his assistant, Genet, had heard the news of Cynthia's death and came to the *bar-salon* briefly to offer their condolences, and then left.

Evelyn, remembering her husband's warning in his letter about Phillip Wingate, might normally have wondered if the Englishman could have killed her daughter, particularly since he would now inherit from her. But Wingate and his sister, Ava, had been present the entire time that Cynthia had been gone from the car, until Julian had discovered her body.

And Phillip Wingate did appear distraught over the death of his bride, in fact, so much so that Ava left the *bar-salon* briefly to get some pills from her compartment for him to take. She returned with the pills while the *Orient Express* was finally making its approach to the end of the journey, snaking its way east over the great causeway spanning the body of water that separates Venice from the mainland.

Marshall, noticing that they would soon arrive in Santa Lucia station, announced that he was going back to get Candace so they would all be together when the train stopped.

He was gone for only a short time before he came hurrying back, highly agitated, to say that Candace was missing from her compartment. And then he pointed to Steven Boland and asked, 'Has he been here the whole time while I was away?'

When the others in the bar car assured him that Boland had been there, Marshall shook his head and could say only, 'Where is she? We must search the train.'

The others agreed. They moved quickly, found the *chef du train*, and had him stop the train while it was still on the causeway only a short distance from the station. That way no one could leave the train.

Once again, with the *chef du train* leading the way, a search was made of all the compartments. There was no trace found of Candace. She had vanished.

Then Evelyn remembered something she had observed while the train had been taking on passengers and baggage back in the Gare d'Austerlitz in Paris.

'There's a huge wooden crate in the baggage car,' she said breathlessly. 'I saw them put it on back in Paris. It's large enough to hold a body! We must check it. Hurry!'

The group rushed forward through the train to the baggage car. There, just as Evelyn had said, was a large wooden crate. The *chef du train* stood with the rest of them for a moment just looking at it. It had been shipped through from Paris, to be picked up in Venice. The name on the tag read: PETERSEN – SANTA LUCIA STATION – VENICE.

'Well, open it, man!' Julian ordered.

The *chef du train* hesitated for a moment more, then shrugged, got a crowbar from the baggage car's tool kit, and prised open the wooden top.

The others crowded close around as the top came up. Inside, the case was empty. There was a sigh of disappointment from the group.

The wooden case was indeed strange, though, as they all noted. Besides being absolutely empty, the case had small holes – which could have been meant as air holes – near the bottom. If, as they could see, the case had not been used to conceal a body inside it, it might still have been meant for that purpose.

A few minutes later the train was moving slowly forward again and then was, at last, stopped and standing in the Venice station.

The Venice police immediately came aboard the train and, after hearing of the murder of Cynthia and the disappearance of Candace, detained all the passengers for questioning.

It was not until a long time later – and after the interrogation had turned up no further clues to the murder or the disappearance — that all the passengers were allowed to leave the train.

II

When, after several days had passed, it became apparent that the police were not likely to make any immediate progress in solving the two mysteries aboard the *Orient Express,* all of those in the Robins party decided to return to London.

Once there, and while awaiting some word from the authorities in Venice, they took up residence in various locations. Evelyn moved into the flat Robins Cosmetics maintained in London for the use of the family. John Forbes and Julian Shields stayed at a hotel. Marshall and Lewis shared the flat where Candace and Cynthia had lived. And Phillip Wingate returned to his flat in London while Ava went to Meadlands. Paul Bryce had flown back to America from Venice. Evelyn had had no further conversations with Bryce, nor did she want to pursue the matter of his settlement with Robins Cosmetics at this particular time.

Julian Shields remained in contact, by phone, with the police in Venice. At the end of two weeks the only information they were able to report to him was that no one had come forward to claim the strange wooden case which had been on the train.

Evelyn and John Forbes and Julian Shields spent most of their time together in London. They were there simply to see if the police in Venice would uncover any new developments in the death of

Cynthia and the disappearance of Candace — in which case they would return to Venice.

Lewis stayed on in London primarily to continue his courtship of Ava Wingate and they saw one another almost every day or evening, frequently in the company of Phillip or of Evelyn, John and Julian.

Marshall was the only one who had a clear and definite purpose for being in London. He believed that Steven Boland, despite all the evidence to the contrary, was somehow connected to the disappearance of Candace from the train. Boland had returned from Venice as soon as the police there had released hm from questioning in the events. And Marshall had had no trouble in tracking Boland down in London.

Marshall soon discovered that Steven Boland ran with a mod crowd in London, his male friends being mostly young musicians, would-be artists, young men in advertising. The young women in the group were a mixture of models and pretty single girls whose parents supported them. There was much partying, at clubs and in the various places where they lived. Boland himself had a studio in a converted warehouse near London Docks which was the scene for many of the parties, lasting all night and sometimes for several nights and days at a stretch.

When he first started following Boland, Marshall had no particular plan in mind. And, for a while, he tried to keep Boland from knowing that he was being followed. Then, after a time, when Boland caught on and spotted him, Marshall decided to change his strategy and deliberately put himself in view for Boland to see him whenever possible. He wanted to wage a war of nerves with the young Englishman.

This strategy worked. And eventually Boland began to make attempts to confront Marshall. Repeatedly, when Boland would spot Marshall following him, Boland would rush up to him, enraged, shouting, 'Why are you bothering me? Stay away! Stay away!' Marshall's response was to shrug and walk away but then, always, to return and resume his shadowing. It was Marshall's hope to wear the other man down or to force him into some kind of action.

One day during this time Evelyn received a mysterious telephone call at her flat. The caller, a woman, identified herself as Lena Bram. She was, she said, a spiritualist. She claimed to have been receiving messages from — as she put it — 'the other side', from Cynthia. According to the spiritualist, Cynthia was anxious to contact her family and friends and had picked her, Lena Bram, to serve as the medium through which to transmit her message.

The spiritualist proposed to Evelyn that a séance be held at the flat where Cynthia had lived with Candace and to have present as many as possible of the family and friends who were on the *Orient Express* at the time of Cynthia's death.

Evelyn was, of course, sceptical of the whole business. But she told the woman she would think it over, took her telephone number, and said she would ring her back after a time.

Later, Evelyn related the story of the phone call to John, Julian, Marshall and Lewis, and to Phillip Wingate and Ava. All agreed that the spiritualist was undoubtedly a fake who had read the stories about Cynthia in the papers, and was probably seeking publicity for herself. Yet they all expressed curiosity as to what the experience of such a séance would be like, a curiosity that Evelyn, too, admitted she felt. It would, at any rate, be harmless enough, they all thought.

Evelyn phoned the spiritualist and said that, yes, she and her family and friends were agreeable to the séance. A date was set for two nights later.

On the night of the séance, Evelyn, John, Julian, Marshall, Lewis, Phillip Wingate and Ava were all gathered at the flat when Lena Bram arrived promptly at the time they'd set.

Evelyn had known from the woman's accent on the phone that she was European. In fact, as Lena Bram told them in introducing herself, she was a native of Transylvania (a statement that those present who were familiar with Gothic tales were sure was pure invention). Mrs Lena Bram was her name, she said.

The spiritualist was a middle-aged, dumpy woman with frizzy cinnamon-coloured hair, a moon face, and great pop eyes. She wasted little time with her talk; instead, she busily directed them into seats around the small dining table in the flat, with herself at the head of the table.

Once they had all taken their places, she went around the room, closing the curtains at the windows and then turning off the lights so that the room was pitch black before she sat down.

For a moment there was silence and darkness until she lit a candle set in a holder, both of which she had been carrying on her person, and placed the flickering candle and holder in front of her.

'Silence!' she commanded, closed her eyes, and bowed her head.

For a long time nothing happened. The candle burned slowly down; there was no sound in the room except, here and there, the squeak of a chair as one or another of those around the table stirred restlessly. And then, suddenly, from the direction of the woman — whose face was hidden beyond the light of the candle — came an eerie hissing sound which built in pitch and finally ended. Almost immediately a disembodied voice spoke, without a trace of an accent, from beyond the candle's light:

'If you would find my sister remember the wooden case on the train. It did not contain a person after she disappeared — but before. Hiding there, unseen aboard the train. And then emerging, snatching her away, and leaping with her from the train. Remember the wooden case. Its mystery is solved. . . .'

The voice died away into the eerie hissing sound again. And once again there was silence. The silence went on. The candle burned lower. There was more restless stirring around the table. Someone coughed. The silence went on. Finally, there was the sound of Julian Shields's voice asking from the darkness: 'Is there anything else, Mrs Bram — ?'

Scarcely had he got the words out of his mouth when the table around which they were all sitting began to lift violently into the air and crash to the floor, lift and crash, again and again, and in the midst of this chaos, came again a voice from the direction of the spiritualist, shadowed in the darkness, a cry, really, gutteral, shrieking:

64

'He—e—e—e—e
kil—l—l—e—e—ed
me—e—e—e—e—'

The candle went out. The table overturned.

'Turn on the lights!' Julian shouted.

Lewis was the first one to reach the light switch. Brightness flooded the room.

The table lay on its side. The spiritualist, Lena Bram, lay on her back. The others who had been sitting around the table were pressing back against the walls on either side of the overturned table.

'Look at her!' Ava said, pointing to the spiritualist. The woman had flecks of blood at the corners of her mouth.

John Forbes rushed to her, felt for a pulse, then said, 'She's alive. It appears she's in shock. Or fainted.'

The others watched while John Forbes rubbed her wrists and lifted her head and moved it from side to side until she finally opened her eyes.

'Are you all right?' John asked.

After a hesitation, the woman nodded her head and then sat up slowly.

John helped her to her feet and to a chair. After he had seated her, he looked around. 'Brandy? Is there any brandy in the place?'

'I'll see,' Lewis said and left the room, returning with a bottle of brandy and a glass. The spiritualist had taken a handkerchief from her pocket, dabbed at her lips, and did not seem surprised when she looked at the blood on the handkerchief. She had bitten her own tongue.

She took the glass of brandy John poured for her, drank, and then looked around at them, a thin smile on her lips.

'Yes,' she nodded. 'I make contact, all right. No joke.'

She took another drink of brandy and, nodding her head wearily, said she wanted to tell all of them something.

What she told them next was that the first part of the séance was an act, a performance. Everything she had supposedly repeated about the strange wooden box on the train she had been told to say, she confessed.

She explained that she had received a letter, with money in it, which told her to arrange the séance and to repeat the message about the wooden box. The exact wording had been in the letter. The writer of the letter promised that if she did have the séance and repeat the message about the box she would receive a second payment of money by mail.

Having told them that part of her story, the woman then held up a hand. 'Wait. There's more,' she said.

The events that occurred next in the séance, she told them, had been beyond her control. 'Sometimes happens,' she said simply. The overturning of the table, the strange voice issuing from her lips had not been an act, she swore. Her 'gift', as she called it, had really worked, as it sometimes did.

She tried to describe what she was sensing during that portion of the séance. She said she could feel a *presence* struggling to speak, to communicate. 'Was this girl, Cynthia.' But the presence couldn't get through, she said, except for the three words they'd all heard. 'He killed me.'

No one in the room knew quite what to make of the woman's story. But it was clear to them that

Lena Bram at least believed what she told them was true.

Julian Shields thought to ask if she would let him have the letter she'd received and also let them know if she heard again from the writer or received additional payments of money. She agreed to both his requests.

After she had gone, the rest of them stayed on in the flat, speculating upon what it all meant.

Most of them agreed that whoever had written the letter to the spiritualist either did know something about an unknown person who had hidden in the wooden case on the train and later abducted Candace — or had written the letter so there would be a séance in which they would all hear about the wooden case, as a way of directing suspicion away from himself.

As to what had happened toward the end of the séance, the most reasonable, realistic explanation they could think of was that some form of kinetic energy had been unleashed in the room, which had resulted in the table moving erratically. And that the spiritualist had psyched herself into a trance in which she imagined, and repeated, words being spoken to her. Or — and they didn't even want to consider this possibility — the woman had actually made contact with Cynthia beyond the grave.

The next day, Lena Bram sent Julian Shields the letter she said she had received. The letter was hand printed on a sheet of ordinary stationery. The message of the letter was exactly what the spiritualist had reported: it said money was enclosed, instructed her to set up a séance with the Robins family, told her precisely what to say at the séance, and promised more money later.

Julian took the letter to a handwriting expert in London, who was unable to give him any help, and to the police, who weren't really interested, and sent a copy of it to the authorities in Venice. There the matter rested.

Ten days later, Evelyn, Julian and John Forbes — taking Cynthia's body with them — returned to the United States. Marshall and Lewis had decided to remain in London for a time.

Cynthia was buried in the small cemetery in the Green Spring Valley of Maryland near the family estate.

In the weeks that followed, the family received occasional reports from the police in Venice that their investigation of the twin mysteries aboard the *Orient Express* was continuing. But no charges or arrests were ever made, and there has been no solution to either case to this day.

NOTES

NOTES

NOTES

CHAPTER FOUR

Copy of a statement made by Henry Fowles to Inspector Robert Covington, New Scotland Yard:

I first got involved in what has since become known as the Lewis Robins case when I received a phone call at my office, requesting me to come to the Robins Cosmetics Company here in London. The caller identified himself as Lewis Robins.

That was about three months ago. I met with Mr Lewis Robins and he hired me to conduct an investigation of a Phillip Wingate. At that first meeting he did not tell me specifically what he wanted to know about Wingate. His instructions were to see what I could find out about Wingate, his business and personal life, his background.

Of course I knew, from the newspapers, that Lewis Robins's sister had been briefly married to Wingate and that she had been murdered during a recent trip on the *Orient Express*. But Mr Robins made no mention of this at the first meeting we had, and neither did I.

For the next several days I followed Wingate closely, day and night, and began to browse in the antique shop he owns and runs on Regent Street. I also began digging into various legal records –

driver's licences, marriage licences, company accounts, property deeds, and the like — to see what I could find about Wingate.

At first everything about the man appeared ordinary, even dull — Wait, I do make one exception to that. I mean, of course, the matter of his first wife's death. There had been no secret about it — it was in the back issues of all the London papers — an unexplained fall she had had, which killed her. Still, with the business of the death of Wingate's second wife, the Robins girl, well . . .

Other than that, as I said, at first everything about Wingate appeared to be exactly as it looked on the surface. For the most part, he kept very regular hours, in the shop in the daytime, at home at night in the flat he had in Eaton Square, with now and then a run out to his house, Meadlands. I found out that his sister, who is quite beautiful, lived most of the time at Meadlands, although she frequently stayed at the flat, too. Her name, I managed to discover, was Ava. I might mention here that I observed Lewis Robins with Wingate and his sister often. It was clear that Robins was very interested in the Wingate woman.

So, I thought, that was why he had hired me to make the investigation. He — Robins, that is — wanted to know more about the Wingate family before he became too involved with the girl.

Now then, during all this time that I was following Wingate closely, I continued to go through such legal records as I could find pertaining to Wingate. While I was engaged in this activity, a very puzzling fact began to emerge. There was nothing wrong with what was in the records. But I slowly began to comprehend that things weren't there that should have been. For example, I began to discover that there was nothing, absolutely nothing, existing anywhere in the records about Phillip Wingate until five years ago — not even, when I got around to looking for it, a record of his birth.

Quite naturally, this struck me as — ah — exceedingly odd. Especially so when I considered that you people, the police, must have encountered this discrepancy at the time you investigated Wingate with regard to his wife's death. What to make of this, I didn't know.

When I reported this piece of information to Lewis Robins, he too found it most unusual. But neither of us had the foggiest idea of whether this fact was important or not.

At this second meeting with Lewis Robins, he confided in me that he was convinced that Wingate had been responsible for his, Robins's, sister's death, even though there was no proof. He wanted me to continue the investigation to see if I could make a connection between Wingate and anyone else who might have been on the *Orient Express* at the time Cynthia Robins was killed. 'I know he was the one behind my sister's murder,' Lewis Robins told me. 'And he's not going to get away with it, even if I have to take matters into my own hands.'

So I went on following Wingate, watching him closely day and night. And this time I concentrated on everyone he came into contact with as well.

I spent time checking out various people who came to his shop more than once, and people who visited him or his sister at their flat or at Meadlands. Most of it was a waste of time.

But there was one chap who caught my eye. It seemed to me he was appearing at the shop, at the Wingate flat, and at Meadlands, on a more or less regular basis.

'Hullo!' I said to myself. 'Let's see about this chap.'

I switched my routine then for a while and began following *him*. The first thing I noticed was that he was with Phillip Wingate or Ava Wingate only when nobody else was around.

To make a long story short, it didn't take me long to find out that this chap worked at Cheltenham — the government's main electronic intelligence centre, as you know.

Well, that made me think a bit but it seemed awfully fanciful to me to make any conjectures at that point about anything. Still, I kept following him. Took me a bit longer to get his name — Colin Strickland. Once I had his name, I went back to the record files to dig into *his* background, and from there to visit places where the records showed he'd lived in the past, and to talk to people there.

I have to digress here and say that whenever I'm on an investigation, I always take photographs — secretly and with a hidden camera, of course — of all the subjects I think might be important to the investigation. So, when I began asking questions of people who lived in Strickland's old haunts, they'd always mention that he had a sister. People I talked to about Strickland always made a big point of telling me that he and his sister were very close.

Well, that confused me for a while because in all

the time I followed him I never saw him with *any* woman — except of course for Ava Wingate. When that thought occurred to me, back to the files I went to look for Ava Wingate's certificate of birth. Again, as in the case of Phillip Wingate, there was no record of birth. There was, however, a birth certificate on file for an Ava Strickland, and according to the date on it, she would be about the same age as Ava Wingate. Naturally, back to Strickland's old haunts I went, this time showing people I talked to a photograph of Ava Wingate.

Yes, that did it. People identified as Ava Strickland the woman who called herself Ava Wingate.

Even with this information in hand — which I didn't yet impart to Lewis Robins — I still didn't know what it all meant. I went on doing the only thing I could think to do, alternate my time between following Phillip Wingate and following Colin Strickland.

It was while I was engaged in this pursuit that I stumbled upon a fact I had failed to note in my earlier surveillance of Wingate and his shop: directly after almost every meeting between Wingate and Colin Strickland, a man — the same man — would visit the antique shop and go away with some purchase or other. The man was a rather elderly, portly sort of fellow.

Once again, I made a switch in my plans, and started following him. He was the first one in the case who seemed to take precautions against being followed — even though he never spotted me. He did, however, lead me on a fast, convoluted trail, and actually managed to lose me that first time.

For the next week I kept a close eye on Wingate's shop until the portly gentleman showed up again.

I watched him leave with his usual purchase, and this time I managed to stay close on his heels. He led me, finally, to his real destination which, as you know, was the Russian Embassy.

Of course, at that moment, I had a pretty good idea of what was going on. But I had no chance to put the pieces together. Because, scarcely had I watched him go through the doors of the embassy, when these two big blokes appeared on either side of me, grabbed me by the arms, shoved me into a waiting car, and whisked me away. I tell you, Inspector, I thought I was a goner. For sure.

The two blokes had got into the car behind me. They forced me down to the floor so I couldn't see where we were going, and we sped off. I don't know how long the ride took but it seemed forever. And then we stopped and I was hauled out of the car, across the pavement, and into a dark building so fast I couldn't see anything.

In the building, with the two of them on either side of me, we went up in a lift, got out, and they prodded me into this tiny office that only had a few chairs in it and a wooden table. They sat me down in one chair, took up positions across the table from me, and began to question me. Their questions came at me like machine-gun bullets.

Who was I? Why was I following the man who had entered the embassy? Why had I been at Wingate's antique shop when the man appeared there? What did I know about what was going on? Who was I working for? Who — what — what — who — ? As fast as I answered one question, they asked another. I admit I was rattled and I told them everything I was doing, everything I knew. And I don't excuse myself for revealing that Lewis

Robins had hired me, and why. I should have kept him out of it, as my client.

They demanded my identification. I gave it to them, and one of them took it and went away for a long time. Checking on me, I guessed. I felt a little better then, not much, because I thought if they'd been Russian agents, they wouldn't have troubled to check up on whether or not I was telling the truth. They'd just finish me off if they wanted me out of the way.

The one who had gone off to check my identification came back eventually, tossed my wallet to me, and nodded his head.

Then they told me who they were: SIS, British Secret Intelligence Service. A couple of MI6 boys, I knew.

They didn't bother to be polite about what they had to tell me: I was to stop following, and forget Phillip Wingate, and anybody connected with him. I was involved, innocently though it might have been, in a matter of national security. I was not to tell anyone else that it was a matter of national security, under threat of prison, but I was to resign the case of investigating Phillip Wingate. And I *was* to warn my client, Lewis Robins, that it would be dangerous for him to pursue his attempt to check upon Wingate. That much I was not only permitted to do, but was urged to do.

They drove me back to my office and released me. And I still didn't know where I'd been.

The next day, I saw Lewis Robins, told him I was bowing out of the case, and warned him in the strongest possible terms that he should forget Phillip Wingate and go home to America.

Robins didn't take too kindly to what I had to

say. He probably thought I'd been bought off by somebody else.

The only problem was that Lewis Robins informed me that he intended to end the whole business with Wingate that same night. That he was going to have a showdown with Wingate because he was convinced that Wingate was out to kill him, Robins. Well, Inspector, I attempted as hard as I knew how to talk some sense into Robins but I knew he wasn't listening.

When I left him, I was extremely agitated. I felt by then I owed the American *something*. So, despite the warning from the MI6 chaps, I determined to follow Lewis Robins that evening. After all, they hadn't said I shouldn't keep an eye on *him*.

I hung around outside the Robins Cosmetics offices until well after dark, when at last Lewis Robins appeared on the street, got into his car, and drove away. I followed in my car, at a distance. Robins drove straight to Wingate's flat. Wingate was waiting in front of the house and got into Robins's car. They drove away and I again followed, again at a distance.

They headed toward the docks. I was far enough behind to see that another car was also following them, a car with one man in it, which kept ahead of me.

What happened as the car with Robins and Wingate neared the docks, you well know.

There was this horrendous explosion and a great ball of flame erupted, completely engulfing the car. It was clear that both Robins and Wingate were consumed by the flames without a chance to escape.

I tarried only long enough to see if I could make out who was in the second car before it drove away. Later as you know, from photographs I was shown here at Scotland Yard, I was able to identify the man in the second car as Lewis Robins's brother, Marshall Robins. Though I have been interrogated repeatedly, I have no answer as to why Marshall Robins was driving Wingate's car. I was told that Marshall Robins explained to your people that he was asked by Wingate to follow in his, Wingate's, car so that Wingate could drive himself back after he and Lewis Robins finished their talk. As far as I know, that could be the truth.

To conclude this statement, I haven't the foggiest notion who killed Lewis Robins and Phillip Wingate. I say that, realising of course that I'd have to be a fool not to have caught on that Phillip Wingate was a KGB agent. That he had been uncovered by the SIS and — although he never suspected it — left untouched so our people could keep up with what his Russian contacts were doing in England. That would explain why the police wouldn't have been too eager to pursue the circumstances of his first wife's death, even if they suspected he did kill her. Or of his second wife's death, although I understand that there were plenty of witnesses aboard the *Orient Express* who testified that he personally could not have committed that one.

Yes, sir, I understand that I am not to discuss any of these matters with anyone, or even think upon them. The SIS people told me the same thing when they informed me that this fellow, Colin Strickland, and his sister, Ava, had both fled the country after Wingate and Lewis Robins were killed.

Beyond what I've said, I wouldn't know what to think about who planted the bomb in Lewis Robins's car that night.

NOTES

NOTES

CHAPTER FIVE

I

She saw him snatch up the sofa pillow and knew with sudden, certain horror that he meant to kill her. The thought filtered through her mind, absurd as it seemed in the midst of her terror, that she could hear in the background the radio playing a recording of 'Laura'.

'Oh — ' she whispered and her 'no' would have been a piercing shriek if the word hadn't been stifled in her throat as the pillow was thrust into her face, smothering the word and her breathing.

She fought back desperately, her body sliding forward off the sofa until she lay on the floor, the pillow jammed into her face. She bit into the pillow, trying to find air, and ripped off some of the pillow's fabric covering with her teeth. She was getting dizzy, yet she kept trying to twist her head from side to side. He kept the pressure on. She couldn't breathe at all. Her body gave one, last convulsive jerk and she was dead. . . .

Her body wasn't found until the next morning. The housekeeper-cook found the body, in the living room, when she came to the house about 8 a.m. to start work. The housekeeper, Mrs Margaret

Carmody, was hysterical when she called the police to report what she had discovered.

The police arrived fifteen minutes after the housekeeper phoned.

The body lay on the floor, fully clothed, a pillow covering the face.

Homicide Detective William Raylor was in charge of the case. There were three other policemen with him — another homicide detective and two patrolmen.

Raylor, after determining that the woman on the floor was dead, asked the housekeeper: 'Who was she?'

'The lady of the house,' Mrs Carmody answered, dabbing at her eyes with a handkerchief. 'Mrs Pittman, her name was. Mrs Libby Pittman.'

Raylor gave orders quickly then. The other homicide detective was instructed to go out to the squad car and call for the coroner and the forensic unit; one of the patrolmen was ordered to go with Mrs Carmody to the phone and see if other members of the family could be located, told of the murder, and asked to come to the house.

Raylor himself went on an inspection tour downstairs and up. The place was a shambles. Drawers had been pulled open everywhere, papers strewn about, clothing flung on the floor, desks and chests overturned, suits and dresses yanked out of cupboards and left in heaps on the floor.

For the next couple of hours the police were busy at the house, taking photographs, dusting for fingerprints, examining the corpse. The coroner gave an estimated time of death between 6 p.m. and midnight — a time that would later be verified when the autopsy on the body was completed at

85

the morgue. Lieutenant Raylor had been anxious to get an estimated time of death before he talked to the husband and the other members of the victim's family who began appearing at the house.

Marshall Robins had been the first one located by the housekeeper when she made her series of phone calls to the family, and he was the first to reach the house. Evelyn Robins, accompanied by Julian Shields, had been the next to appear, followed soon after by John Forbes. George Pittman, Libby's husband, did not get home until an hour later; he had been out of town during the previous night and hadn't known of the tragedy until he called home in late afternoon.

Once they were all there, Raylor began to discuss the case by saying: 'From all the initial evidence we have come across, this would seem to be a case of burglary — of breaking and entering — by one or more persons who may have been surprised in the act by Mrs Pittman. And so she was killed.'

He paused to observe the effect his words were having on his listeners.

'Actually,' he went on, 'bearing out the possibility that this is what happened is the fact that this particular area has been the target for a series of such breakings and enterings recently. We have had five such incidents in the past month. Fortunately, in the other cases, no one was home at the time or walked in while the crime was in progress, so there was no violence involved.'

'I don't believe that's what happened here!' Evelyn interrupted loudly.

Lieutenant Raylor crossed to her quickly. 'Why do you say that?'

Evelyn just shook her head without answering, and when Raylor repeated his question, Julian Shields spoke up, 'Lieutenant, Mrs Robins here has been through a traumatic period in the past several months — '

Julian had taken Raylor by the arm and walked him to another part of the room where he briefly explained about the series of murders which had wiped out members of the Robins family one by one in the course of a year.

'All right, I understand,' the police lieutenant said when Julian finished speaking, 'but I'm not satisfied that there may not be more to this murder than a burglary. Despite what I told all of you a few minutes ago.'

'Other than that outburst by Mrs Robins,' Julian said, curious, 'why would you think there's anything suspicious about Libby Pittman's death? To my eye, it certainly looks like someone broke in and burgled the house. And then, as you said, she surprised them in the act.'

'Yes, it looks almost too much that way,' Raylor said slowly.

Julian frowned. 'I don't think I understand what you're getting at.'

The lieutenant said softly, 'Did you ever hear ot the phrase "red herrings"?'

'Yes, of course.' The lawyer nodded.

'Meaning,' Raylor said, 'that somebody goes to a lot of trouble to make it look like something happened in a certain way, when it didn't happen that way at all.' He glanced around the room. 'Well, that was one of the things that occurred to me when I first inspected the house. Now, after what you've told me about the deaths in the

87

Robins family, I'm — well, suspicious.'

The detective didn't have any more than that to go on for the moment, but he did decide to question each of the persons now at the house as to where they had been the night before, particularly between 6 p.m. and midnight.

Both Julian Shields and Dr John Forbes had been miles away in New York City, and both had witnesses who, they said, could place them there for all of the evening before. Shields had been at dinner with a client of his, and then at the theatre with the same client. Forbes had been with Evelyn Robins, having escorted her to a concert at Lincoln Center, after which they had had a late supper.

Marshall Robins, as it turned out, was supposed to have had dinner with his sister Libby, who was now dead. According to his story, he had come here to the house about 8 p.m. to take her out, but the house was dark and there was no answer when he rang the bell and knocked on the door. Also, her car was missing from the driveway and the garage. He said he'd waited for half an hour to forty-five minutes, hoping she'd show up. He knew that his brother-in-law, George Pittman, was out of town — which was the reason he was taking Libby out to dinner — and he didn't know who else to call to ask where she might be. He had finally left, concerned but not deeply worried, and driven back to the city. He had stayed at the apartment of Lewis Robins, which he had been using ever since Lewis had died and he, Marshall, had returned from England.

George Pittman had been in Washington, D.C., overnight, a fact he could verify. The only problem Lieutenant Raylor had with George Pittman's story was that Pittman could have left the house close enough to 6 p.m. to have killed his wife and still have arrived in Washington at the time he said he did.

The homicide detective had left Evelyn until the last to question. Her own time had already been accounted for by John Forbes, but Raylor wanted to know about her earlier outburst — 'I don't believe that's what happened here' — when he had said that a burglar could have killed Libby Pittman.

'I probably shouldn't have said anything, Lieutenant,' Evelyn said, slowly. 'I have no proof of what I think, and so I suppose I shouldn't make accusations which I can't back up.'

Raylor smiled at her reassuringly. 'You can speak freely to me, Mrs Robins. This is an investigation of a murder case. The only way we're going to solve it is to accumulate all the facts we can and try to come up with the truth. Now, please tell me what you think.'

Evelyn nodded. 'What I think is that my daughter was killed by one of my late husband's exemployees. A man named Ernest Truax.'

She then went on to explain that some months before, her husband, Tyler Robins, had discovered that Truax was selling information to a competitive cosmetics company about new products being developed by Robins Cosmetics. She told him how her husband had approached the head of the rival company and — the way she worded it — 'had asked for a settlement of damages'.

After Tyler Robins was killed, she continued, the head of the rival company had indicated he would pay the damages rather than go into court. However, within the past few weeks this man had changed his mind. Robins Cosmetics had therefore started a legal action, and the case would soon be heard.

'And exactly where did your daughter fit into all this?' the lieutenant asked.

'She was to be the main witness,' Evelyn said. 'She worked in the same department with Ernest Truax and was the one who first found out that Truax was stealing and selling information about Robins Cosmetics products. There is other evidence. But my daughter's testimony was, I believe, crucial to the case. And so do my attorneys.'

'We'll check this Ernest Truax out carefully,' Raylor said firmly.

William Raylor was an intelligent, dedicated police officer and for the next several weeks worked day and night to solve the murder of Libby Pittman.

He had hoped that the forensic lab people would be able to aid his investigation but they came up empty-handed. No incriminating prints were found in the house: there were prints of George Pittman and of Marshall Robins, as well as of other members, or friends, of the family, but they could be explained as having been left at another time.

The lieutenant was especially disappointed that the sofa pillow found with the body had yielded no clues at all. Not only could they find no traces of a possible murderer on the pillow but the pillow was oddly lacking any traces of the victim: no spittle, no marks, no prints. The police considered the possibility that an entirely different object might have caused her death by suffocation, but a thorough search of the house failed to turn up any such object.

Because of the manner in which other members of the family had been killed in a relatively brief period of time, the lieutenant did not exclude the possibility that Libby Pittman might have been murdered by one of her family or friends. He interrogated them relentlessly, especially the husband, George, and the brother, Marshall. Again, although he could not exclude either of them as possible suspects, neither could he place either of them inside the house at the time of the murder.

One thing that did occur was that George Pittman, in the course of his interrogation, hinted strongly that he believed his brother-in-law, Marshall, had killed Libby. According to George Pittman, Marshall and Libby had quarrelled over business affairs, over the board of directors of Robins Cosmetics. As Pittman told the story, after so many of the other members of the family — who had served on the board — were killed, Libby felt that her husband, George Pittman, should have a place on the board, as a member of the family by marriage. Marshall had opposed this. On the night Libby and Marshall were to dine together, George Pittman said, Libby was going to tell Marshall that Evelyn was prepared to side with her in the matter. With only three votes remaining on the board — Evelyn's, Libby's and Marshall's — Libby would get her way. Also, George Pittman pointed out, Marshall was the one, single member of the family who had been present when each of the other members — Tyler, James, Cynthia, Candace and Lewis — had been killed or had disappeared.

Even with this information, Lieutenant Raylor was not able to develop any real evidence that Marshall was responsible for his sister's death.

Finally, with the suspect Ernest Truax, who perhaps had the best motive for murdering Libby Pittman, Raylor fared no better. Even though, in a diary Libby Pittman carried, police found an entry: *Truax 8 p.m.*

In the case of Truax, there was simply no way the police could connect him to the crime because of the time element, the period between 6 p.m. and midnight. The autopsy had conclusively fixed that as the time of the murder.

And for that period of time, on the night of the murder, Ernest Truax had a houseful of witnesses who swore that he had not left the premises, located some five miles away from the Pittmans, during the hours between 6 p.m. and midnight. Truax had been giving a party at his house that night, and it had begun at 5:30 p.m. and continued until 1 a.m. While no one at the party could swear where Truax was every second of the time, all were able to swear that he was never out of sight for the time it would have taken to drive to the Pittman house and back. When questioned about the entry Libby Pittman had made in her diary — *Truax 8 p.m.* — he did say that Libby had phoned him at that time and had said she wanted to talk to him the following day. So Lieutenant Raylor had reached a dead end with his most likely suspect.

II

During the course of the investigation of Libby Pittman's murder, Lieutenant Raylor — as a routine part of his job — questioned all those who lived in the area of the Pittman house. There were no close neighbours, the nearest house being a few hundred yards away. It was in this house that the lieutenant was to encounter a Miss Agnes Ellsworth who was to supply him with an endless number of possible leads in the case – and an equal number of headaches.

On the first day that he visited Agnes Ellsworth, shortly after Libby Pittman's body was found, the neighbour seemed to have an encyclopaedic knowledge of the George and Libby Pittman family.

'Such a tragedy,' she said to Raylor when he informed her of Libby's death. 'But then, they were always so *busy* that I suppose it was inevitable that something would happen to one or another of them.'

The remark struck Raylor as exceedingly strange, but his experience in questioning possible witnesses in police matters was that they often blurted out comments at first meeting which they hadn't intended to say. And that if they were interrogated too closely on the remark, they were made wary.

So Raylor said nothing in reply and, instead, appraised the woman carefully.

Agnes Ellsworth was of medium height, white-haired, with a cheerful, ruddy-cheeked face. Her green eyes had a bright, pixielike twinkle. The lieutenant guessed her to be a spinster from a family that had had some money, both speculations later borne out when he checked into her background.

Her house was neat, spotless, and there was a beautiful rose garden outside the windows of the sun porch where they sat talking.

'I didn't know the Pittmans all that well,' Agnes Ellsworth said, 'but from what I saw of the comings and goings over there, particularly in recent days, I thought, goodness, something must be up.' She looked at Raylor bright-eyed, and added, 'And now you tell me there's been a murder. My!'

The lieutenant glanced out of the window as he said, 'You say you noticed the comings and goings at the Pittman house. Can you really see that much of their place from here?'

Miss Ellsworth nodded. And then she said she hoped he wouldn't think that she was just a nosy busy-body but that she would show him how she observed the Pittman house. She then led him upstairs to a large, airy bedroom on the second floor. 'My room,' she said.

She went to a window facing toward the Pittman house, with Raylor following. On the sill of the window was a pair of high-powered binoculars. She picked them up, glanced through the lenses, and passed them to the lieutenant. 'Look for yourself.'

When Raylor held the binoculars to his eyes, he was startled to see how the distant house and grounds came into close-up focus.

Miss Ellsworth made no apologies for her use of the binoculars to peer at her neighbours, saying, 'I read in the papers where a lot of the police departments in the cities encourage citizens to become what they call "neighbourhood watchers", even supplying many of them with binoculars. That's where I got the idea. I thought somebody ought to keep an eye on things hereabouts.'

'All right,' Raylor said. 'Now, tell me, did you

notice anything unusual at the Pittman house on the night of the murder?'

'No.' She shook her head. 'I wasn't watching the house at the time.'

She went on to say, 'You can be certain that I'd have paid closer attention if I'd had any idea of what was going on over there.'

'I'm sure you would,' the lieutenant agreed. Then he questioned her about her earlier statement, that the Pittmans were always so busy that she had supposed it was inevitable that something would happen to one or other of them.

She explained that in all the time she and the Pittmans had been neighbours they had seemed to lead a somewhat quiet, routine life, both of them home almost every evening, early, at about the same time. And that she hardly ever noticed anyone visiting them.

'But in recent days,' she said, 'I noticed a man visiting there, actually visiting Mrs Pittman in the afternoons when she came home from work for a while; then this man would leave, and she'd leave.'

Lieutenant Raylor didn't quite know what to make of the incident. But he asked Miss Ellsworth to describe the man as best she could.

She was able to supply him with a rather general description, which he noted in his book. Then he thanked her for her help and asked that she let him know if she recalled anything else, or saw anything else.

'Oh, indeed I will,' she said delightedly. 'Why, I feel almost like a detective myself.'

In coming days, Lieutenant Raylor learned for himself just how much Miss Ellsworth did fancy herself a detective.

Almost every day from then on, the woman was on the phone to him, proposing a possible new theory. That Libby Pittman was having an affair with the man who had come to the house in the afternoons. That the man's wife had found out about it and killed her, or had her killed. That George Pittman had found out about the affair and had killed her or had her killed.

Lieutenant Raylor did follow up on these leads but all of Miss Ellsworth's theories turned out to be wrong when he discovered, from the description supplied by her, that the man who had visited Libby Pittman in the afternoons was B. J. Grieg, the Robins family's private investigator. Furthermore, George Pittman had known of the visits all along. When Raylor questioned Grieg, the private investigator said that Libby Pittman had used his services to check on Ernest Truax, the man she was going to testify against at the trial. Grieg did not, however, have any information on Truax that would connect him with her death.

In addition to interrogating Ernest Truax, Raylor had also had several long sessions with Paul Bryce. Since Bryce had also been at the party given by Ernest Truax — and had witnesses who swore he had been present during the 6 p.m. to midnight time period fixed by the autopsy for the murder — he had to be eliminated as a suspect.

There was one development in the case, ten days after the murder, that had Raylor hoping it was about to be solved. A burglar was caught ransacking a house a couple of miles away from the Pittman residence. The burglar was a thirty-five-year-old ex-convict, Tony Spadua. Police were convinced he was the one who had been breaking into all the houses in the area and they worked hard to tie him to the killing of Libby Pittman.

The lieutenant brought Miss Ellsworth in to view a line-up in which Tony Spadua stood with seven other men. She did pick Spadua out as looking like the man she'd seen lurking around the Pittman house in the days before the murder. Unfortunately, she picked out an additional man who turned out to be a police detective. Raylor did not feel he could rely with confidence on her ID of Spadua.

Nevertheless, the police worked hard to tie Spadua to the murder of Libby Pittman. Raylor, along with a team of detectives, interrogated the ex-convict relentlessly. A couple of times while they were grilling him, Raylor was sure that Spadua was about to crack and confess.

And then this lead, too, ended inconclusively when one morning Tony Spadua was found dead in his cell with his wrists slashed.

Lieutenant Raylor was never able to shake off his instinctive feeling that the killer of Libby Pittman had created a trail of red herrings — by making it look as if a robbery had taken place — to cover up the real motive for the murder. But he still wasn't able to come up with proof as to the identity of the killer and so the case remained open but unsolved in police records.

For Libby's funeral, George Pittman again designed the tombstone which covered her grave in the small cemetery in the Green Spring Valley.

Some days after the funeral, George Pittman announced that he was going to create, and himself construct, a special family monument to be placed in the cemetery. This particular monument

would contain various objects and articles connected with the dead members of the family, much
like an ancient Egyptian pyramid. The monument
would then honour all the departed members of
the family, even those whose bodies were missing,
such as Tyler Robins.

Evelyn and Marshall visited George while he
was still in the early stages of planning the
monument. It was to be a massive affair, a huge,
hollow construction, covered over in marble, and
George was doing all the work on it alone.

Evelyn thought it a weird undertaking on
George's part but she supposed he was doing it to
assuage his grief over the death of his wife, and
said nothing.

NOTES

NOTES

NOTES

CHAPTER SIX

I

There were ten of them on the island.

Dr John Forbes was the host. He had discovered the island on a previous trip to the area and, for their holiday, had rented the only house there, a massive stone castle affair which sat like a fortress in the centre of the one-mile-square spot of land jutting up out of the sea. The structure had tiers of rooms rising to an open turret on top.

The ten of them were: the host John Forbes, Evelyn Robins and Julian Shields, Marshall, George Pittman, James Robins's French widow, Geneviève, the Robins butler and housekeeper, Alfred and Dorina Wales, and two surprise guests.

John Forbes had said that part of the reason for the holiday would be to celebrate the forthcoming wedding of Evelyn Robins and Julian Shields. The two of them had spent much time together running the business of Robins Cosmetics since Tyler Robins's death. But still, the announcement that they planned to marry caught most of those who knew them by surprise. John Forbes, who must have foreseen the marriage, had accepted it with seeming good grace, and had insisted upon the island holiday.

They had arrived together by launch from the mainland after a jet flight from home. The launch would return every three days to bring supplies and take off anyone who wanted to make the return trip during the month they planned to be there.

John had made arrangements beforehand with some people on the mainland who had seen to it that the place was in readiness when they all got there. From then on, Dorina and Alfred had attended to the cooking and household chores.

'It's such a lovely place, so peaceful here,' Evelyn had said, kissing John on the cheek. 'It was so thoughtful of you to plan this trip.'

Marshall's opinion of the place, on the other hand, as he whispered jokingly to Geneviève, was, 'It looks like Dracula's castle.'

In truth, the place did have a dark, forbidding feel to it at night – isolated, with its dozens of rooms closed and silent above the sweeping spiral staircase which wound around and around from the first-floor entrance hall up to the lofty turret.

By daylight, however, the island was bathed in sunlight, the sky cloudless, the sea sparkling.

Most days they all swam in the sea, sunned themselves, read, ate too much, and, in the evenings, watched movies on the projector they'd brought or played word games. Evelyn and Julian frequently strolled the island, hand in hand, like teenagers.

Not long after they all began their holiday idyll, it became apparent to the others that Marshall and Geneviève, James's widow, were developing a relationship. A month earlier, Marshall and Pamela, the wife from whom he was separated, had finally divorced. Geneviève had left her baby in France.

Evelyn was extremely unhappy about the growing closeness between her son and daughter-in-law. She expressed her displeasure to Marshall, and even suggested that he return home, but he refused to listen to her.

Marshall was unhappy because of two other circumstances as well. One was the tension that existed between him and George Pittman, a tension Marshall had first sensed after Libby's death. But George had never said what it was that was on his mind.

The other circumstance that distressed Marshall was the forthcoming marriage of his mother to Julian Shields. Now that there was no one left in the family to whom he could talk about his concern, he confided in John Forbes.

'I think everything between Julian and my mother just happened too fast,' Marshall said. 'When they marry, I know he means to take over Robins Cosmetics. In fact, he's already managed to get her to give him power of attorney in her business affairs. I worry that he may be a shrewd opportunist.'

'Are you worried about your mother, or the business?' John asked bluntly.

'Both,' Marshall answered candidly.

John nodded. 'Fair enough. Have you tried to talk to her about this?'

Marshall shook his head. 'What good would it do? She's already down on me enough because of my feelings for Geneviève.'

'Your mother,' John said matter-of-factly, 'is a

very romantic person. But I think you're wrong about Julian. Unfortunately. I say unfortunately because if you were correct, there'd still be a chance for me. As it is, I truly believe they're deeply and sincerely in love with one another. More's the pity for me.'

The two surprise guests John Forbes had invited on the holiday were there to supply entertainment for the others. The two were Joachim, the magician, and his assistant, Genet, who had been aboard the *Orient Express* at the time Cynthia was killed.

When he started planning the holiday, John Forbes had sought out the magician and his assistant, found them between engagements, and hired them to come to the island for a couple of days to perform for his friends.

It did not escape the notice of those present that John Forbes seemed quite taken with Genet and found every excuse possible to be with her. She was indeed a beauty and appeared to like John Forbes. However, Evelyn, in particular, could see that Joachim was trying to conceal his displeasure at the growing relationship between his assistant and John Forbes, although Forbes gave no sign of being aware of the magician's feelings.

On the evening when John Forbes had arranged for a performance by Joachim, all the guests gathered in the drawing-room, sitting in a circle of chairs, in the centre of which Genet had placed a small platform and a cloth-covered table. She then set up a spotlight to illuminate the platform and the faces of the group gathered to watch. All the other lights in the room were turned out, and when all was in readiness, Joachim entered and stepped up onto the platform.

He was attired in a dinner-jacket over which he

wore a long black opera cape with a scarlet lining. The girl stood beside him, dressed in an ankle-length black gown and wearing around her neck a glittering diamond choker that caught and reflected shafts of light. The effect of the two of them was mesmerizing.

Joachim made a formal bow toward his audience and then stood erect, his hands upraised as his long, elegant fingers moved rapidly in the air. Genet repeated his message aloud:

'Joachim say it is great pleasure to be here to perform for you tonight. He say magic you will see now is like life . . . all is illusion. He thank you for your attention.'

The magician removed his cape and placed it on the table, and his fingers moved rapidly again as the girl asked if someone in the room would hand them a book from one of the shelves near the fireplace.

Evelyn went to a shelf, took down a book, and brought it to Joachim. He took the book in his hands, riffled through its pages to show nothing was concealed there, then handed the book to Genet. While she stood holding the book, he lifted the black cape from the table, swished it through the air, and let the cape tumble to the floor as he reached a hand up into the darkness above the pool of spotlight and plucked a single red rose out of the air.

He took the book from the girl, put it on the table, opened the book — placed the rose inside it — and closed the book. Then he swirled the cape over the book and the rose, and the rose disappeared. Genet handed the book back down from the platform to Evelyn, saying, 'He say please hold.'

106

Once more Joachim's fingers moved rapidly and Genet translated: 'He say now would lady speak aloud a page number in book.'

Evelyn nodded and said: 'Page forty-five.'

'Joachim say please open book to page,' Genet said.

Evelyn nodded again, opened the book to page 45 and gave an exclamation of pleasure as she lifted out a rose petal.

Following Genet's instruction the book was passed from person to person, each announcing a page number before receiving the book, each lifting out a rose petal when the book was opened to the announced page.

The group applauded Joachim and Genet.

The magician went on for an hour creating his illusions, all of which held his audience enthralled, especially three acts of his magic that left them completely mystified.

In one, Joachim took a deck of cards and flung them high into the air, out of sight above the beam of the spotlight. While the cards were out of sight in the air, Genet asked anyone in the audience to call out a card.

Marshall responded, saying loudly: 'The queen of spades.'

As they all watched, a single card fluttered down out of the overhead darkness and landed face up on the platform: the queen of spades.

For a moment there was silence in the room as they all waited for the rest of the cards to come tumbling down. When, finally, they realized no other cards would appear, they all laughed and applauded.

In another, perhaps the most impressive illusion of the evening, Joachim asked John Forbes to step up onto the platform and take a seat in a straight-backed chair. Genet, who had left the platform briefly, returned with a long, gleaming sabre which she handed to Joachim. The magician held the sabre in one hand and with his other hand lifted his cape from the table and draped it over John Forbes so it completely covered him. There was a startled gasp from those watching as, almost as soon as the cape had settled over John Forbes in the chair, Joachim raised the sabre and thrust it straight into the cape, the end of the sabre protruding from the back of the chair.

Moving swiftly, Joachim reached forward and pulled the folds of the cape back over the hilt of the sabre, the blade of which was then revealed to be piercing through the bones of a skeleton, bringing another gasp from the group watching.

Joachim bowed to his audience, turned, flung the cape over the mound on the chair, withdrew the sabre, and lifted the cape away to show John Forbes sitting in the chair, blinking his eyes. The magician shook the cape out, holding it high, so the group could see there was no hole in it where the sabre had been thrust through it. There was more applause. Afterwards, when John Forbes was asked how the trick had been performed — where he had been moved when he was replaced by the skeleton — he claimed not to know. All he did was shake his head in seemingly honest bafflement, explaining that he had no memory of anything after he sat in the chair, that perhaps he had been hypnotized. Also he said that he honestly wondered if Joachim wasn't really and truly an alchemist. Nobody believed John Forbes, however, thinking that he was just going along with the act.

The third act of magic Joachim performed that

completely mystified the group was also the final act of the evening's performance. This time Joachim swirled his cape back and forth in front of the audience and, one after another, countless fully inflated coloured balloons floated out and up into the air. The group, enchanted, applauded until Genet turned on all the lights to reveal the whole drawing-room filled with brightly coloured balloons. They were all captivated by this delightful conclusion to the magician's performance.

After taking his bows, Joachim once more raised his hands and moved his fingers rapidly, Genet putting the sign language into words:

'Joachim say enjoy the magic of life. Thank you.'

Afterwards everyone in the room gathered around the magician and his assistant and showered them with compliments.

John Forbes was pleased with the success of the evening's entertainment.

II

The following morning Evelyn decided to visit the mainland since the launch was due at the island that day. She wanted to do some shopping. Julian went with her.

In the early evening, when the launch brought Evelyn and Julian back to the island, a storm had blown up. A heavy rain was falling, high winds swept across the island, and the sea crashed up against the shore. After depositing Evelyn and Julian at the island's dock, the launch quickly departed before the storm grew worse. Evelyn and Julian were loaded down with shopping bags containing purchases they'd made, including an expensive pair of gold cufflinks for John Forbes.

But as soon as they reached the house, thankful to be out of the storm, Evelyn and Julian discovered that a mystery had occurred during their absence: John Forbes had not been seen since mid-morning, and although the others at the house had made a complete search of the small island, no trace of him could be found.

'We've looked everywhere,' Marshall said wearily. 'I don't know where he could be. And there's no way he could have left the island. No other boats have been here, except for the launch.'

'Have you searched the whole house?' Julian asked.

'Not everywhere,' Marshall answered. 'As you know, several of the rooms on the upper floors are locked. We did bang on the doors of those rooms and call out to ask if he was inside. But why would he be in any of them? And we did look in all the other rooms.'

'Well,' Julian said grimly, 'we're just going to have to break down the doors to those rooms that are locked. If there's a chance he's inside one of them, we have to find him. There's nothing else we can do since the launch won't return for another three days.'

While the men prepared to go through the house, breaking down doors where need be, Evelyn, worried and confused, went to her room to change her clothes. When she opened a drawer to take out a blouse, she noticed her diary there and a piece of paper sticking out from between the pages of the diary.

She took out the paper, filled with a feeling of foreboding, and unfolded it with trembling fingers.

The words were typewritten and unsigned. The note read:

Dear Evelyn:
This is to say goodbye forever. I will not say more. I am taking my own life.

John Elliot Forbes

Evelyn hurried back to the others and showed them the note, saying, 'I don't believe John would take his own life. Oh, he couldn't do that! It must be a joke or a trick.'

'Oh my,' Julian said, shaking his head. 'This is terrible. We must contact the police as soon as possible. I suggest that we try to get through this night as well as we can and tomorrow attempt to catch the attention of a passing boat and send word to the mainland for the police.'

A short while later the storm grew worse and all the lights on the island went out. They all agreed it would be useless to try to search the house in the darkness and that they would wait until morning and hope they could get a message to the police.

None of them could eat any dinner that evening, and after sitting around in the living-room in the gloom and candlelight, while outside the storm raged for long hours, all retired to their bedrooms.

Evelyn tried to write in her diary:

I don't know what to think or say — John, John, John — why? why? why? I'm so sorry —

At daybreak the storm had passed, and they were all up and scattered around the island, anxiously searching the waters for sight of a passing boat.

A few minutes before noon, Alfred managed to catch the attention of a small yacht which was

111

going by only a few yards offshore. Through frantic waving motions, he was able, finally, to convey a distress signal. The people on the yacht — it later turned out that they were an English couple on holiday — sent over a rubber dinghy, with two crewmen in it. Julian explained to them what had happened and asked them to get word to the mainland that the police were needed. The crewmen said that they would see to it.

Later, while all those on the island were awaiting the arrival of the police, Evelyn was restless and began prowling through the big old house, finally reaching the open turret at the top, from which she could see the water spread out on all sides of the island.

While she stood on the turret, her eye was caught by an inscription engraved in stone, set into a section of wall. It was only a single line of letters which she assumed had been left by some former inhabitant of the ancient fortresslike house:

TO ETTITI MOY

As she was leaning forward, trying to puzzle out the letters, she felt a terrible, hard blow strike her violently across the back. She screamed and screamed as she pitched forward, her body arching high out over the waist-high parapet encircling the turret, and then she was falling down, down . . .

Geneviève was outside the house, walking towards the sea, when she heard Evelyn's first terrible scream. Geneviève looked up in time to see Evelyn's body as she fell over the top of the parapet and then watched, in speechless horror, as the body plunged earthward, hit, and lay unmoving.

The poor girl screamed for help and dashed towards where Evelyn lay, hoping against all reasonable hope that she was still alive. But of course after the fall from such a great height Evelyn was dead.

All the others, who had been inside the house at the time, rushed out, attracted by Geneviève's screams. As soon as they saw for themselves that Evelyn was dead and there was nothing they could do for her, they wandered away dazed and shocked. Only Julian remained, head bowed, beside her body.

Because the police had been sent for earlier, it wasn't long after that they arrived from the mainland. The police had come thinking they were going to deal with a suicide, only to find themselves with another body on their hands. Even so, they dealt with both incidents in the most perfunctory manner. It was clear that they had little interest in these outsiders from other parts who came there and caused trouble by committing suicide and falling off buildings.

The police did of course take a statement from Geneviève that she had witnessed Evelyn's fall. And they did question everyone on the island as to where they had been at the time of the fall. That questioning led nowhere since all the others said they had been inside the house, in different rooms, and so knew nothing about what had happened. Further, since Geneviève said that as far as she had been able to see there had been no one else in sight in the turret, the police seemed satisfied to accept Evelyn's death as due to an accidental fall. And the case was closed.

After the police were given John Forbes's suicide note, they began a search through the house for

113

his body. By sundown that day they still hadn't found him and they postponed the search overnight.

While the police were still on the island, the others decided they didn't want to remain there any longer and packed and left with the police when they went, taking Evelyn's body with them. On the mainland Joachim and Genet left for Paris while the others booked into a hotel. The police took Evelyn's body away for a routine autopsy.

Several more days passed, while the group remained at the hotel, before the police finally found John Forbes's body hanging by the neck from a rope in the corner of a storage cellar beneath the house.

By that time, the police had released Evelyn's body. The autopsy showed she had died as a result of injuries suffered in her fall. The group flew home with Evelyn's body. She, too, was buried in the family plot in the cemetery in the Green Spring Valley of Maryland.

The police held John Forbes's body for autopsy. Then, after it was determined that he had died by hanging, the police shipped his body to his home in Illinois where he was buried by a sister.

NOTES

NOTES

CHAPTER SEVEN

I

After Evelyn's death, Marshall Robins — the last surviving member of the Tyler Robins family — stayed on at the Greenlawn estate, frequently commuting to the Robins Cosmetics headquarters in New York City or to the laboratories in New Jersey. Although Marshall now held the title of president and chairman of the board of the company, he had come to rely more and more on Julian Shields to run the actual operation.

Alfred and Dorina Wales were also at Greenlawn, serving Marshall as butler and housekeeper-cook. Geneviève had spent some time at the estate with Marshall, immediately after Evelyn's funeral, but had since returned to Paris.

From then on, Marshall led a somewhat solitary life and seemed to be more and more preoccupied with his own thoughts.

And then yet another curious incident occurred, of a kind that seemed to dog the footsteps of all who bore the Robins name. Early on an autumn morning, Marshall Robins's car, a Bentley, was found overturned in a shallow ravine beside a

117

country road some eleven miles from the Green-lawn estate. A passing truck driver discovered the wrecked car and, using a CB radio, called the state police.

When the police reached the scene, they could find no trace of Marshall. But they did spot what looked like two bullet holes in the windows of the overturned car, one hole in the Bentley's rear window and one in the window on the driver's side of the car. When the lab technicians and the homicide detectives called in by the patrolmen reached the scene, it was verified that the holes in the windows had been caused by bullets. Despite this evidence, there was no sign of blood any-where — in the interior of the car or outside it.

This time, a captain in the homicide division of the state police was put in charge of the investi-gation. His name was Waltham. Detective Sergeant Horgan, who had headed up the earlier investi-gation of the shooting of James Robins at Green-lawn, entered this case as assistant to Captain Waltham. Waltham was of medium height and build, in his forties, an intense man, impatient and demanding.

'I want this case solved,' he announced as soon as he had seen the car and found that it had belonged to Marshall Robins. 'One after another the members of this family have been done away with, with no solutions as to who did it, when, where, how, or why — this time I want answers and I mean to get them.'

With those words, Waltham, accompanied by Sergeant Horgan and several state troopers, went to Greenlawn.

There, Alfred and Dorina appeared to be shocked when told of the finding of Marshall's car, of the bullet holes in the car's windows and of the disappearance of the man himself.

'All we can tell you,' Alfred said in answer to Captain Waltham's questions, 'is that Mr Marshall Robins had been in New York City for the past several days and must have been driving here from the airport when it happened. Mr Robins often arrived unannounced so I cannot tell you when he might have left the airport, whether last night or early this morning.'

The police stayed on at the house, making phone calls to check on Marshall Robins's movements during the past twenty-four hours. In a phone call to the Robins Cosmetics headquarters in Manhattan, Waltham verified that Marshall had been there the day before. The homicide captain spoke with Julian Shields, who told him that Marshall had planned to leave New York the previous evening to return to Greenlawn. Julian also said that he himself would be flying down to the Maryland estate as soon as possible, since he wanted to be present as the Robins lawyer.

Another phone call to the local airport turned up the information that Marshall Robins had flown in by a private charter plane the night before, arriving at the airport — located almost twenty miles from the Greenlawn estate — at approximately midnight. Marshall kept his car parked at the airport while he was on trips to New York, and several witnesses said they had seen him leave the airport in the Bentley soon after midnight.

Captain Waltham phoned in to the state police barracks and instructed them to send out an all-points bulletin on Marshall. The captain also obtained from the butler and the housekeeper a photograph of the missing man to give to the newspapers and television stations.

Waltham had been questioning Alfred and Dorina in the living-room of the house and was prepared to leave when Sergeant Horgan came into the room. Horgan had thought of checking out the gun case, which he remembered from his earlier visit to the estate, and had slipped away and gone to look around the library where James had been shot. Now the sergeant took Waltham aside to announce that one of the weapons in the gun case in the library seemed to be missing.

The captain and Horgan went to the library, accompanied by Alfred and Dorina. In the gun case, as the sergeant had reported, there was an empty place in a tray that contained a collection of revolvers.

'Do you know anything about this?' Waltham, turning, demanded of Alfred.

'No, no, sir,' Alfred answered, shaking his head.

'There is a gun missing, right?' The captain took a step towards the butler.

'Yes. It would appear so,' Alfred agreed. 'Yes, that tray was always filled. But I know nothing of this — '

Waltham twirled around swiftly towards Dorina. 'And you? Did you notice that a gun was gone from here?'

Dorina had shrunk back from Waltham, in fear.

'Captain,' Alfred said quickly, 'she wouldn't notice. Dorina never goes near any of the guns. She's terrified of them.'

Waltham looked at Alfred for a moment and said, 'All right, a gun is gone. Somebody took it. And somebody shot at Mr Robins's car.' He pointed a finger at the butler. 'Did you leave the house last evening, early this morning?'

Alfred, too, was now genuinely frightened. 'I —' he said falteringly, and stopped.

'*Did you?*' Waltham demanded.

Alfred glanced nervously from the captain to the sergeant. 'I — yes. This morning, early, I drove the Volkswagen to a filling station down the road to get gas. Last night Dorina said she needed some things from the store and we were going shopping later today.'

Waltham looked at him hard. 'You said this was early. How early?'

'About — about seven a.m.' Alfred said.

'I told you where Mr Robins's car was found,' the captain said. 'How far is the filling station from that spot, would you say?'

The butler looked worried. 'About — approximately two — three — miles I would guess. That is, from what you've told me, Mr Robins's car was found about two or three miles on the other side of the filling station from here.'

'I see,' Waltham said, and making a quick decision, added, 'I'd like you to come to the police barracks with us and give us a signed statement.'

'No!' Dorina cried out.

Alfred went to his wife to comfort her, saying, 'It's all right, Dorina. I won't be gone long. It'll be all right. You'll see.' He glanced at Waltham and then at Horgan and said to his wife, 'When Mr Shields arrives, if I'm not back, tell him what's happened and ask him if he will come to help me.'

They left the estate, Captain Waltham and Sergeant Horgan riding with Alfred in one of the patrol cars.

At the police barracks, the butler was taken to one of the interrogation rooms. There Captain Waltham continued to question him, not only about the events of the previous night and the morning but of the past mysterious deaths of the members of the Robins family. Alfred kept answering that he had told the truth about what he had done that morning, and that he knew nothing about the other deaths that the police didn't already know.

Despite the butler's denials, Waltham kept up the interrogation through the morning and into the afternoon until, just before evening, Julian Shields arrived.

The lawyer quickly came to Alfred's defence, saying to Captain Waltham, 'Look here, sir, you have no right to continue to hold this man and badger him as you have been doing. Now, I demand that you release him.'

'Of course,' Waltham said smoothly. 'I was only questioning him as a witness. Now, if he'll read and sign a statement which I have written down, he'll be free to go.'

'Good,' Julian Shields said curtly.

Alfred, relieved, went to the cloakrooms for a wash while Waltham gave his notes to a police clerk to type up, and then the captain came back into the interrogation room to speak with Julian Shields alone.

'Mr Shields,' Waltham said, 'I'm confident you must be as anxious as the police all over the world to clear up the mysteries of the deaths of the Robins family.'

'Of course I am,' Julian said coolly. 'But I am also a lawyer, the Robins family lawyer, and I intend to see to it that their interests, and the interests of anyone connected to them, are protected.'

The captain frowned. 'Even if I told you that I think it's possible that Alfred Wales might hold the key to the solutions of all their deaths?'

'Oh, come on, now,' Julian said impatiently. 'You can't seriously mean that you think Alfred — why, he wasn't even present when some of them died or disappeared.'

'Let's look at it another way,' Waltham said. 'He *was* present when most of them did, including — I might remind you — the most recent and the last remaining member, Mr Marshall Robins, this morning. Now, if I can just find a motive, well — '

Julian shook his head. 'I think you're on the wrong track.'

'We'll see,' Captain Waltham said. 'I'm letting him go now. But I intend to continue this investigation. And I will be talking to him in the near future.'

Julian shrugged.

Alfred returned to the room. After Julian carefully read over the statement Waltham had prepared and gave his okay, Alfred signed the paper. The lawyer and the butler left the police barracks.

Captain Waltham, fired with ambition and believing he might be close to solving a string of murders, wrote a press release on the disappearance of Marshall Robins and gave it, along with a copy of Marshall's photograph, to the newspapers and television stations.

II

The next day, newspapers and TV news shows all around the world carried an account of the police press release and Marshall's picture, asking HAVE

YOU SEEN THIS MAN? All the stories included a quote from an unidentified source: 'Police have a definite suspect in the case.' The enigma of the earlier fate of the members of the Robins family — now coupled with the strange disappearance of Marshall Robins — captured the public's curiosity around the globe.

As a result of the widespread news stories, the police were soon inundated with reports from citizens who believed they had seen the missing man. A cab driver in Manhattan claimed he had taken Marshall Robins from JFK Airport to the city. A woman in California said she had seen him on a trolley bus in San Francisco. A truck driver in Maryland was positive he had given Marshall a lift in from the Green Spring Valley to Baltimore. A motorist in Virginia had picked up a hitchhiker he thought was Marshall and had driven him to Delaware. There also were reports that he had been spotted in London, in Paris, in Rome and in Texas, among other places.

Captain Waltham didn't believe any of these stories. He was convinced that Marshall Robins was dead, probably buried somewhere, and that Alfred Wales was his murderer. So positive was he that he had the butler brought in for another session of questions, hoping to break him down.

Julian Shields accompanied Alfred and sat in on the interrogation. This time the lawyer allowed the police captain to question Alfred without interfering, while still making sure the butler's rights were not violated.

The truth was that the lawyer himself had begun to have some doubts about Alfred. The seed of his doubt had been planted by a remark made by Waltham when he had talked with Julian alone the first time they'd met, the remark the police captain had made about finding a motive for Alfred to want Marshall dead.

Julian, as the Robins family lawyer, of course knew of the financial arrangements Evelyn had made for Alfred's daughter and her baby by James Robins. Sooner or later, as the last remaining family member, Marshall would find out about these arrangements. Julian knew that Alfred would be able to figure this out. And the question Julian kept asking himself was: would Alfred — in fear that Marshall might try to cut off the financial arrangements once he knew about them — kill Marshall? The question troubled the lawyer.

And so, while he said nothing to Captain Waltham of this possible motive, Julian was interested in having the police find out all they could about the butler.

Alfred, for his part, must have sensed the subtle change in the lawyer's attitude because, as the interrogation progressed this time, Alfred began to lose his confidence. As Waltham went over and over the various deaths of the members of the Robins family, of James, Cynthia, Lewis, Libby, Evelyn, of the disappearances of Tyler, Candace and now Marshall, Alfred's responses became more and more muddled, almost evasive. And he was exhibiting other, visible signs of distress or guilt. The sweat was pouring off him, his hands were trembling, his voice was croaking.

Finally, Waltham paused in the interrogation, beckoned to Julian to step out of the room with him, and said to the lawyer in a whisper: 'I think he's about to crack.'

Julian could only nod his head.

The two men returned to the room. Alfred,

watching Captain Waltham approach him again, was cowering in his chair.

Then, just as Waltham — sure that Alfred would crack with the next statement — said harshly: 'Tell us the truth, Alfred Wales,' the phone in the room rang.

Waltham snatched up the phone in a rage, yelled, 'Yeah?' and then seemed to collapse at what he heard.

The police captain appeared bewildered, un-believing of his own words when he hung up the phone, turned to Alfred and Julian, and said, 'That was a report from the police in Baltimore. Marshall Robins just walked into police headquarters there. He's alive and unharmed. He said he's been suffering from amnesia. He's on his way here now in a squad car.'

'Are they sure — ?' Julian started to ask.

'They're sure it's him,' Waltham answered in a hoarse voice.

'Mr Marshall, he's alive,' Alfred whispered. 'Oh, thank God.'

It was sometime later before Marshall reached the police barracks. He looked tired, thin and drawn, and was unshaven, his clothes dirty and wrinkled.

He told his story slowly. On the night he had flown in from New York, he had got into his car after midnight and started to drive to Greenlawn. Along the stretch of road where his car later had been found, he had been overtaken by a car coming up fast behind him. Shots had been fired at him and then his car had been forced off the road, overturning in a ditch.

In the darkness he had managed to get out and run and hide. There had been two men in the car.

126

They had searched for him in the darkness, cursing and yelling. He had heard their voices, caught glimpses of them. Both were big men, huge in size. He hadn't seen their faces clearly. He had managed to crawl away from them in the darkness. And then he had run and run and run. The shock had hit him later and he had suffered amnesia, not knowing who he was or where he was. He vaguely remembered catching a ride with a truck driver. He remembered nothing else until today when his memory returned on a street in Baltimore. He had gone to police headquarters and they had told him about the stories in the newspapers and on television. He had called Greenlawn and spoken to Dorina. She had told him the state police were questioning Alfred. He had got the Baltimore police to call the state police and then had come to the barracks. That was all he knew.

The police typed out Marshall's statement and he signed it. Later, he gave such descriptions to police as he could manage of the two men he said had attacked him. No arrests were ever made in the case.

The incident became one more curious chapter in the drama of the Robins family.

NOTES

NOTES

CHAPTER EIGHT

Those who knew Marshall Robins became alarmed over his growing paranoia after the episode of the wrecked car with the bullet holes in the windows.

Marshall now lived alone at the Greenlawn estate in Maryland where he had become a virtual recluse. He had fired Alfred and Dorina Wales and, except for occasional trips into the New York offices of Robins Cosmetics, saw no one.

Marshall had even broken off all ties with Geneviève, to whom he had seemed genuinely attracted. Nor would he have anything to do with his ex-wife, or George Pittman. Julian Shields, who was now running Robins Cosmetics, was the only one ever to talk with Marshall. And Shields, too, had become quite worried about Marshall's condition.

In fact, some weeks after Evelyn's death, Julian had gone to visit George Pittman to discuss what, if anything, could be done to help Marshall.

'George,' Julian said, 'the man needs help. He's totally paranoid, thinks somebody is out to kill him next. He keeps saying there's some kind of sinister plot against the Robins family, to eliminate all of them. Isn't there anything we can do for him?'

George shook his head. 'I don't know. I've spent a lot of time thinking about this whole business with that family, especially Libby's death. Sometimes I wonder if maybe there hasn't been a plot all along to kill them off.'

'But that's impossible,' Julian protested. 'There's been *no* one suspect who's been in or near the scene of the deaths or disappearances when they occurred.'

'Maybe not a solid suspect,' George said. 'But there has been one person present each and every time – Marshall himself.'

'Oh, come on now,' Julian answered sharply. 'You can't possibly think he's done away with all the rest of them.'

George shook his head slowly. 'No, I suppose I can't. Although I have considered the possibility from time to time.'

'Anyhow,' Julian said, 'what are we going to do about Marshall? Can we talk to him?'

'I'm willing to do that,' George agreed. 'On condition that you set it up.'

Julian said he would and, a few days later – after trying to phone Marshall repeatedly and getting no answer – made a visit to the Greenlawn estate in Maryland.

His first view of the place appalled him. The lawns and gardens had grown wild, the swimming pool, still filled with water, gave off a dank cesspit smell, the horse stables were empty, dirt had blown across the tennis courts and, he noted, several windows in the upper floors of the house had been broken.

There was no answer when he rang the bell and pounded on the door. Yet he felt someone was inside the house observing him. He walked around

131

and around the place, calling out Marshall's name, and when, finally, there was no response, he gave up and left.

When Julian reported his experience to George, George said, 'Well, I guess you just have to keep trying. He's probably barricaded himself inside there and won't answer until he's ready.'

Another few days went by and George again received a phone call from Julian. This time the lawyer was highly excited and agitated.

'Listen,' he said, 'I just had a phone call from Marshall. He said he wanted to talk to us, to you and me. He said he had important news to tell us. That it was urgent.'

'All right,' George said, 'I told you I'd talk to him with you – '

'No, wait, listen,' Julian cut in. 'There's more. I told him we'd see him at Greenlawn right away. But he said that wouldn't do. That we'd meet at your house, the three of us, at six o'clock tonight –'

'All right – ' George said again and again Julian cut him short, adding, 'There's more. Just before I got the call from him, I received an audit of Robins Cosmetics books which I ordered a while back – ' he stopped talking.

'And – ?' George asked.

'And,' Julian said slowly and carefully, 'the books show that twenty-five million dollars are missing. I'm trying to have the money traced. So far, we have been able to determine that Marshall transferred at least five million to his personal account and from there to – to God knows where. It looks like he's responsible for taking the whole twenty-five million – '

'And putting it in a Swiss bank account,' George said.

132

'I don't know.' Julian's voice sounded bewildered. Then he said, 'Look, I'll be leaving here shortly. It'll take me that long to get to your house by six.'

'I'll be waiting,' George said.

Actually, it was 6:40 p.m. when Julian reached George Pittman's house. George was waiting for him but there was as yet no sign of Marshall.

'Traffic was terrible coming out here,' Julian said. 'No sign of him, yet, huh?'

George shook his head. 'When he didn't show up, and neither did you, I tried phoning him repeatedly. There was no answer.'

At seven o'clock, when Marshall still hadn't appeared, the two men tried several more times to phone Marshall at Greenlawn. There was no answer.

Finally Julian said, 'Well, there's no other way, we're just going to have to fly down to Maryland and call in the police.'

They rented a charter plane at New Jersey's Teterboro Airport and flew to Maryland. As soon as they were on the ground and had rented a car, Julian called the state police. He identified himself, explained that he was afraid there might be something wrong at the Greenlawn estate, and asked that the police meet him and George Pittman there.

A short while later, when the two men arrived at Greenlawn, the police were already there, waiting in two patrol cars.

Julian and George told the police that they were concerned about Marshall Robins who was, they thought, inside the house.

The police then broke down the door and entered, followed by Julian and George.

The inside of the house looked like a pigsty, with old newspapers, cans of food, dirty dishes everywhere on the lower floors. There was no sign of Marshall, but in a bathroom on the second floor they found a grisly sight: the bath, the shower, the walls and floors were splattered with blood. However, though they searched the house, they were unable to find a body.

Once again, homicide detectives and police technicians invaded the estate to try to collect evidence. Julian and George were taken to the police barracks where they were interrogated and eventually released.

Several more days passed before the police completed their scientific analysis of the evidence they'd found in the house. The most startling fact that they determined was that the copious amount of blood found in the bathroom was of a different type from Marshall Robins's. The blood in the bathroom was type O, and — as police found from Marshall's past medical records — his was type A.

In addition, when the police made a more thorough search of the house, they were unable to turn up any clothes or other wardrobe items that could have been Marshall's.

The blood found in the bathroom of the house at Greenlawn particularly baffled police. And then they discovered, as they widened the investigation, that some weeks earlier a quantity of blood used in experiments at the Robins Cosmetics laboratories in New Jersey had been stolen. Records kept at the laboratories showed that the blood type stolen from there matched the blood type splattered around the bathroom, so the murder scene could have been staged.

Also, as police searched the house more

134

thoroughly, they came across a batch of notes in an envelope, with a rubber band around it.

The notes were unsigned and were composed of letters clipped from newspapers. All the notes read the same:

YOU ARE A MURDERER!
YOU WILL DIE!

There were a dozen such notes and there was no identification of where they had come from, nor how Marshall Robins had received them. The notes were sent to the police laboratory for analysis but the police were unable to pick up any fingerprints from them or any other possible clues as to who had sent them or where they had come from.

And there the investigation as to the fate of Marshall Robins remained, inconclusive.

Some weeks later the skeleton of a female was washed ashore from the Gulf of Trieste along the north-east coast of Italy. Since the skeleton could not be identified through medical or dental records as that of any female reported missing in the area or, eventually, of any female missing in Italy, the report went to Interpol's offices in France.

More time passed until Interpol came up with the name of a female who had vanished in the region a long time before: Candace Robins. A subsequent comparison of Candace Robins's medical and dental records established that the skeleton was indeed hers.

And so, not long afterwards, in a small ceremony attended by George Pittman, Pamela, the ex-wife of Marshall, and Julian Shields, Candace was laid to rest in the cemetery in the Green Spring Valley of Maryland, alongside other members of her family.

There too, that day, George had placed in the family plot the towering monument he had finally completed, to stand as a memorial to the mystery of the deaths or disappearances of the Tyler Robins family.

Engraved on the face of the monument was the inscription:

MEMORIAL STANDING HERE TESTIFIES
BEHIND DEADLY KILLINGS CALCULATE
MURDER PLOTS UNBEKNOWNST
CRIMES CONCEALED MYSTERIES
— 3— 83 —

Within the year Julian Shields married Janice Elgar, who had been on the cruise aboard the Robins's yacht, *Falconer*, when Tyler Robins had met his strange fate. She and Julian Shields had met during the memorial service for Tyler Robins, after the cruise, at Greenlawn. Following the death of Evelyn Robins, Julian Shields and Janice Elgar had started seeing one another in London and the United States and had decided to marry.

After their marriage, they bought the Greenlawn estate, restored it, and went there to live.

NOTES

NOTES